Eccentricity is Pippin Pearmain's lifelong stock-in-trade. She used to be a niche-market performer, but at sixty-six, she hasn't worked in a decade. That doesn't matter to Pip. She has her cosy life at Lemonwood Cottage, an interesting friendship with Mister Clancy next door, walks on the beach and occasional stoushes with the officious and the annoying. She enjoys her regular ballet practice and her daily battle with the bad-tempered lemon tree in the garden.

Pip has two cat companions, and if they choose to communicate with her in Cat-Morse about things no cat should be concerned with, well—no one else needs to know. Above all, she has her green-penned bucket list. That is unique.

An impulsive trip to her old hometown stirs memories for Pip when she meets her cousins Juniper and Lupin at the Delmsford Flower Show. Over a nostalgic afternoon tea provided by the Lilac Ladies in their retro-pinnies, Pip shares a long-held secret with her cousins and is given their secrets in return. Jan's secret is fun. Lupin's secret will be turning Pip's life upside down . . . but not quite yet.

First, she has to negotiate the flower show . . . shuffle her place in the family pack and accept the unexpected gift of Lupin's cat.

Performing Pippin Pearmain 1
Copyright © 2022 Lark Westerly
ISBN: 978-1-4874-3682-7
Cover art by Martine Jardin

Published by eXtasy Books Inc

Look for us online at:
www.eXtasybooks.com

PERFORMING PIPPIN PEARMAIN 1
PERFORMING PIPPIN PEARMAIN

BY

LARK WESTERLY

DEDICATION

For all the eccentric, loving, independent, determined, peculiar, wonderful women everywhere . . . and for those who like them just the way they are.

AUTHOR'S NOTE

Pippin Pearmain appeared as a single mention in *Being Tamzin 7*. Her cousins Lupin and Juniper have never appeared before.

The Blake family appeared in retrospect throughout the *Being Tamzin* series.

Pip's story covers a year, taking her from her reclusive life in her cottage in Jellico Bay to her old hometown of Delmsford, to the magical fossmere, on to Sydney and thence to Delphinium Island. The nine books compile into one continuing story, slowly revealing the mystery and magic that has been part of Pip's world all along.

So—how did I come to write Pip's story? Would you believe, it all began with a bucket?

A Note on Reality

Major places such as Tasmania definitely exist. However, the towns of Delmsford and Jellico Bay are made up. The Lilac Ladies don't exist either, although they bear a slight resemblance to the doughty ladies of the CWA. Their story is partially told in *Anne and the Lilac Ladies Spectacular*. And yes, flower shows with afternoon teas in town halls are still going strong. I went to one this year.

PART ONE. PIP'S BUCKET LIST

February 2022

CHAPTER ONE. QUEUES AND COAL AND CUTTINGS

Pippin Pearmain had a bucket list.

It was a lovely list, recorded in green ink whenever she found a new bucket to add.

The list was her private treasure — something to occupy her mind during those queueing-around-the-block moments or green room marathons that stretched beyond infinity and back again. Not that there had been green room marathons lately — or even snaking queues, now she came to think of it. Jellico Bay, where Pip lived now, was deficient in both.

Still . . . she remembered how it had been.

Other people gossiped in the few short queues there were at the supermarket or at Jelly-and-Juice, or scrolled through their phones, sighed, and glanced at the clock, if there was one. Or they calculated the exact second when the parking meter, still manual in Jellico Bay though terribly outmoded elsewhere, might flick into an accusing triple zero with a decimal point to inform one it was an emergency but not a phone-dialable one if there wasn't . . . a clock in sight, that was. Sometimes even Pip failed to untangle her inner syntax.

Who cared? Little Nanna Laurel had always said Pippin was one out of the box, and suggested they'd broken the mould when she was made. She didn't mention whether that was a good thing or not. Little Nanna loved fiercely, and thoroughly, as she had done all things. The younger Pippin had wanted to be just like Little Nanna Laurel, but she knew she

1

never would be. No one was.

Maybe that was why they got along so well.

Pip hummed happily in queues at a pitch that made some fellow queuers want to rub their ears and blame their tinnitus or a distant mosquito. They never blamed Pip, because she didn't look like a hummer. She was so small and slender that she wore jeans in children's sizes and little shoes that could barely hold coal at Christmas — if she'd ever been bad enough to deserve any.

People had never given Pip coal for Christmas. To her disappointment, they didn't give her chocolate, either.

In the early days, directors wanted to keep her small, slight, and porcelain skinned. Therefore, their *gifts to our little star* were never chocolates, wine — well, of course not — or flowers. These were seen as inappropriate. Instead, they gave her charming seed pearl bracelets with enamel flower dangles. Mostly, the flowers were pink roses. Once, it was an orange marigold. The other regular gift was a high-end plush cat with a diamanté collar. She wore the bracelets to premieres, and sometimes the latest cat went too.

Tiny Pippin Pearmain attends the premiere of The Many Selves of Merry.

Much was made of the fact that she was technically too young to view the film, and so was taken out after the first half hour.

As Pippin grew into her later teens, the directors and casting agents apparently thought she stayed small by rigorous application of a sans-chocolate diet. No longer *our little star* but now *that quirky ingénue*, Pip continued to get the annual bracelets, now set with sapphires, garnets, or aquamarines. The plush cats were eventually discontinued in the early 1980s. Maybe someone noticed Tiny Pippin Pearmain must be nearing thirty. Maybe the cats went out of production. No one explained, and Pip didn't ask.

Much later still, as *that odd little woman — is she still acting?*

Really? she slipped off the directors' Christmas list entirely.

Sorry, Ms Pearmain. The subtext was there, though it remained largely unspoken. *You're not suited to mumsy roles. You're too small to be a love interest. You look odd in chorus lines. You don't suggest Strong Heroine, Va-va-va-voom . . . First Victim, Third Alien,* or *Quirky Aunt, maybe.*

It didn't matter too much. Sully had warned her it would happen. And she was still acting, really, often enough to pay her modest bills. Not that she called it acting. If anyone asked her — these days few people did — Pip said she was a performer.

Pip's waif-like dimensions were nothing to do with self-denial. She would always be small because her grandparents and her parents were all small people. If anyone had bothered to look up and apply the mathematical formula that allows one to calculate probabilities, then the result might have been quite close to Pip's actual height in her little shoes.

Her cousins Lupin and Juniper had Big Nanna de Leon and Little Nanna Laurel for grannies.

Little Nanna Laurel was the granny they shared with Pip.

Pip had Little Nanna Laurel and Little Nanna Pearmain. Both ladies knew the value of wearing shoes that were practical while also tending to diminutive feet and pleasing the soul. They made sure Pip did, too.

Pip had nice feet, slender and high-arched with pretty toes.

Today's shoes were green. They had yellow daisies on them.

Pip wasn't being twee. The shoes were the only green ones she could find that fitted her perfectly. She planned to keep them for a long, *long* time. One of the advantages of staying the same size in perpetuity was the ability to wear clothing until it wore out. One of her favourite pairs of jeans had been purchased in 1979. They had the bell-bottomed silhouette to prove it.

Pip often dressed in green. When she was seven, she'd

been a tree nymph in a naughty Greek play. She hadn't had lines to say. All she had to do was to perch in a tree which had a handy ladder for added balance and peer down at the cavorting characters below.

Now and again, she tried to remember the exact title of the play. She knew she'd gone to lots of rehearsals, but she'd spent much of the time reading stories from her favourite book, which she'd propped in the crook of a branch, well out of camera-range. *Grandmother's Sunshine* always absorbed her attention, but she could snap back to performance mode in less than half a second.

That play—God, it wasn't something by Shakespeare was it? *The Tempest? The Dream?* Surely not. It had Greeks in it. Not Agora-Greeks, she thought, but the Arcadian kind.

She'd loved the green costume she got to wear in the play. The local papers had made special mention of *Tiny Pippin Pearmain, whose wide-eyed avidity was worthy of its own curtain call.*

The reviewers hadn't mentioned the green costume, but it had made itself part of the legend in Pip's mind.

Pip still had the press cuttings somewhere—and the costume, come to that. She even had the plush cat associated with that Christmas bonus—though it didn't have the diamanté collar. Maisie Mink had borrowed the cat at a Possum Club sleepover, and the collar had never come back.

Maybe she could open some boxes and search out the cuttings one day. That would remind her of the play's name, at the very least.

Might ask Sully.

Oh. That's right—I can't.

Pip had been in lots of plays since the one with the Greeks and the tree, but that had been the first. She thought she should remember it better than she did.

Might arrange the cuttings and costume and plush cat in a row and put myself in the middle, she mused. See who's the most faded.

Pip was aware she was fading just a wee bit. Her skin needed a little more Caraway's Loving Lotion than it had. A few of her toenails were less like crescent moons and more like chalk deposits. Her once cornsilk hair now resembled cobwebs of indeterminate colour. It was still soft and fly-away, but the white-gold hue had faded. Her knees had developed a few wrinkles that not even Caraway's Buttermilk Balm could fix.

Pip didn't mind — much. So, she creaked a tiny bit on winter mornings! So did the porch swing, and no one suggested that was over the hill.

Mind you, she thought, there was really no one *to* suggest it — other than the cats.

She didn't feel any different inside, where it mattered. She was Pippin eternal, Pip perpetual, the essential Pippin Pearmain, distilled to the tincture, the elixir, the very essence of Pip.

Some women lost themselves in the welter of life. Pip was sure she became more herself with every passing day. She was even still performing . . . if one counted performing Pippin Pearmain.

Pip did. She gave thanks for that to someone or other. She wasn't sure who it was — but possibly whoever it was had a cat.

Sometimes, she wondered if she could claim the ear of Bastet, but she thought one had to be Egyptian to do that, and she wasn't. The Pearmains and the Laurels had been English before they turned into Australians. She wasn't sure about the de Leons, but they weren't her blood anyway — not directly, although Big Nanna and Big Pop had loved her almost as much as they loved Lupin and Juniper. Big Nanna had stood five feet ten in her bare feet. She had a waist like a barrel, a booming laugh, and the heart to match her girth.

Wee Pippin, she'd called Pip. Or sometimes, she said *the wean,* although she wasn't Scottish.

Pip hummed happily, buzzing through the days and embellishing her bucket list whenever the opportunity arose.

The occasional bucket additions could be ink-translated in kitchen-table communions with a cup of camomile tea. The original cat kept company while Pip wrote, buzzing its approval in medium key.

CHAPTER TWO. FEINT-LINED WITH MENTAL INK

By now the physical iteration of the bucket list occupied sixty-something whole pages of a feint-lined notepad left over from Pip's brief stint as a minute taker for the Delmsford Flower Club.

The minutes were petrified by time, but Pip didn't like to tear them out, in case someone rang her out of the blue, or drove two-and-a-half hours from Delmsford, clopped up onto her porch and rang her bell, squinted at her over menacing specs, and asked for visible verification of whatever decision Oliver White had made about the morning tea at the Delmsford Dahlia Spectacular in 1972.

Scones or pikelets? Dabbled with jam or crimpled with cream? Quince paste or pineapple conserve, and were the biscuits kiss or cherry-titted nibbles?

What?

Maybe he meant cherry jam drops? Had she misheard, trapped by a memory of Pearmain-de-Leon family-speak?

Yes. The notepad was that old. The pen wasn't, though. Pip had given up buying green pens by the post-decimal dozen because by the time she dumped a dry one, the others had gone out of ink in sympathy. These days, the first bloodless scratch of a pen on feint-ruled paper sent her scurrying down Hope Street to Jellico Bay Gifts and Cards to purchase a new green pen.

It was unthinkable to write her bucket list using anything

else.

Now and again, Pip fantasised about making her own ink. She'd even looked up a recipe which called for green leaves, vinegar, salt and a blender. What stumped her was the baby food jar which was apparently the container of choice for storage.

What would she do with the baby food? Feed it to the original cat?

The cat didn't do puree, any more than Pip did. Come to that, she didn't have a blender. She didn't have scissors, either. She thought she probably should get a pair of those.

More to the point, she didn't have a dip pen, or any idea about how to mend a quill. In historical novels the heroines were always mending their quills or passing them to gentlemen to be mended for them.

Back in the day Pip had sat in a mocked-up wooden-panelled manor house library, writing a letter with a dip pen. She'd worn a long green dress with a fichu. She'd written neatly in her minuscule writing, but before she got more than three lines in, the director called *Cut* and got Sully to ask her to *write a bit bigger, so we can get a shot over your shoulder.*

Pip had written *a bit bigger*, but it had still not been big enough.

Sully had laughed and said Pip was a *human typewriter* whose writing matched her stature.

I wish I'd souvenired that dip pen, Pip thought.

There was something else she wished she'd souvenired from the set of *House of Heriot*, but she'd thought she'd better not do that until she was older.

She did have something nice from that time . . . or lots of somethings if she counted her memories of a smiling young man who smelled of freshly made toast. He'd played an actual lute and they'd gone for walks in the garden of the physical set that stood in for the manor exterior.

Oakengrove. That had been the name of the historic home. It had stood not far from a town called Fiddle Bay. He'd told her about the place he lived, in a house like Oakengrove. It was called Barfleur Manor, which seemed very grand to Pip.

"Maybe you'll come to visit one day, Pipkin."

"I'd like that."

"Please do. We could go riding, or maybe go to a ball. Go as ourselves, I mean, not as Marigold and the Highwayman. We could dance all night and go home at sunrise."

"Why sunrise?"

"Sunrise is my favourite colour."

"I wish we could." She'd known even then it probably wouldn't happen.

Filmsets were like that. So were plays.

Hotbed friendships. Sully had warned her of those.

The other actors will pet you and compliment you and make you their mascot. They'll say you're wonderful – and they'll mean it, then. You are wonderful, but when other actors say it then it's similar to the way they call you darling. You'll have lunch with them every day. They'll learn your favourite food and you'll know theirs. You'll have catchphrases that will make you feel like a member of the club. You'll be invited to private suppers. You'll know them very well, then.

Next time they see you, they might wave and smile, and call you darling, but they won't remember your real name.

Next play, next film, next pet, next mascot.

Don't take it to heart.

It's harmless if you know the rules and never mistake it for anything real.

That's the way it goes with hotbed friendships.

"Do you really wish for that?" Her co-star had favoured her with his most delightful smile.

"I really do." She'd smiled back. She'd meant it, whether he did or not.

"Then it will happen. One day, when you're older."

"One day."

That conversation had been fifty years ago. Their *one day* had never come.

Pip had never ridden with him again. She'd never danced with him at an unscripted manor ball or walked home with him in the sunrise. She'd never again worn a fichu or written a letter with a fine dip pen.

Anyway, a biro was good enough for writing a bucket list. Was there really a jazz singer named Bickerson Biro, or was she making that up?

Must check next time I go to the music library. Maybe when I want a change from Ness MacConnel and Evgeny Drozdov. Though jazz mightn't go too well with ballet.

Pip loved her bucket list dearly. It was her go-to friend — her memo to the past, her pleasant present and her hopes for a future that would be more of the same.

She thought everyone should have one . . . a bucket list *and* a hope for the future.

So — why, she wondered, didn't she share her list with anyone other than the cat?

CHAPTER THREE. CAT-MORSE AND A SENTIENT LEMON

Pip wondered on a regular basis why she shared her bucket list with only the original cat. She usually concluded it was because she was a miser. She hoarded shoes and memories, long-ago newspaper cuttings and, until the futility assailed her, packets of ten green pens with one dry, one on duty, and the others gently leaking their lifeblood into the air one molecule at a time.

And there she went again.

Her mind was a frog, a cricket, a grasshopper, or maybe a vegetarian flea. It hopped off in random directions whensoever it chose.

They might call that ACDC these days, Pip mused, then she wondered if that was the term she meant. Wasn't that a band, or an electric shock?

She asked the cat for an opinion.

The cat blinked a slow-motion reply.

Cat-Morse. Is that a thing?

Pip was sure she didn't have ACDC, although she allowed she might be a bit—but *only* a bit—OCD. She could concentrate if she chose. She didn't absolutely *have* to do her ballet practice at seven-on-the-dot each weekday morning *or* drink a cup of hot water with eye-watering lemon juice pressed from a savage lemon at eight o'clock.

She didn't *have* to go adventuring to the tank garden each morning to choose that sacrificial lemon.

It wasn't the end of the world if she failed to blow a kiss to the camomile or jerk her chin at the sly-eyed gooseberry bush that played Charybdis to the sentient lemon's Scylla.

Green pens — pffft! She could write in blue or black or even electric gold if she chose. She simply hadn't chosen to yet.

What she had was an active mind. She had an athletic brain, busy doing aerobics in her skull. Or maybe it was more like those urban adventurists who hurtled themselves around the neighbourhood, skateboarding down banisters, bounding from gutter to gutter, ducking and weaving and clattering along the rooftops like Spring-heeled Jack.

The bucket list was an island of calm, growing steadily like a plant in the sunshine of creation in her fairy-sized writing.

Maybe I could tell the back-up cat, Pip thought, eyeing that animal as it rolled on the deeply grooved boards of the porch.

The original cat blinked Cat-Morse to show it disagreed.

The back-up cat was too young to be entrusted with such important information.

Tell it when I'm gone where good cats go, signalled the cat. *That will ease its sorrow and give it a sense of the baton passing — the gravity of responsible knowledge for the feline repository.*

Really? Would the back-up cat feel sorrow? Pip had thought the cat and the back-up had barely noticed one another's existence in the few months since the back-up had materialised in her camomile garden.

She'd barely noticed the original cat at first.

Ten years ago, she'd brought her bruised and frozen self to heal in Lemonwood Cottage at Jellico Bay. She'd been there for six days when she finally realised her eyes were *not* deceiving her brain in the matter of the cat.

They deceived her a lot in those days.

Little Mum Rosie had never been to Lemonwood Cottage, but Pip's eyes insisted on seeing her there, kneeling in the grass with her floral gardening gloves and her white hair bundled under a straw hat with traverse stripes of green and blue.

12

Pip's ears joined in from time to time, convincing her brain for a second or so that Little Mum was with her in the garden.

Put the kettle on Pipsi-pola. Call me when it boils. By the way, did you post off my order to the folk at Kleine Nederlanden?

You're not here, Little Mum. There's no point in posting your order now.

Those firebird tulips they offer are something I've never seen before. They'll wake up the old garden!

Little Mum, please. That garden isn't ours any more. Now I have a new one.

You do? But why? Sorry, love, of course you need to do what's best for you. I just wish you had some company. You should go back out into the world.

I will. I promise. I need a little while, that's all.

It was almost a relief to Pip when she started seeing the original cat in her new home instead of Little Mum.

Company.

Pip had moved to Jellico Bay because remaining in Delmsford had become Too Much. Pip always thought of that state with initial capitals. People kept asking, inviting, calling, suggesting — it was kindly-intended but Too Much. They brought flowers, which was ridiculous because Little Mum's green thumbs were legendary. If Pip had wanted flowers in the house, she could have stepped out to pick some.

These were your mum's favourites. Don't they remind you of her?

If Pip had wanted to be reminded, she'd have gone out and stood on the arched wooden bridge and watched the goldfish go by.

Little Mum had never understood those goldfish. She said *she* had never put them in the pond. Where *did* they come from?

Pip could have told her, but now it was too late.

People brought casseroles in two-eared covered dishes. They brought tuna bake with pasta.

Pip thanked them distractedly and buried the food in the garden.

She felt a bit guilty, but why should one small, bereaved woman plod through a week's worth of meals she didn't like?

She washed the dishes, scrubbing off baked-on tuna, and set them on the porch with thank-you notes.

She made herself toast and tea, but she didn't put the tea in her favourite cup.

That would have been Too Much. Sometimes even the toast was Too Much and made her cry.

Too Much wasn't to be borne, so Pip didn't try.

She fled to—no! It wasn't a fleeing. It was an ordered re-treat. Or maybe it was really an advance, to a place where Too Much was left in her wake.

In my dust. That was better. Someone else could tend the old home garden and puzzle over the giant goldfish with white splotches on their orange hides.

Someone else. Pip didn't know who. She didn't want to. She put the matter in an agent's hands and *advanced* to Jellico Bay.

For six days Pip sat in her new cottage while the dust set-tled and the wake rippled into nothing but gentle calming seas.

The real sea swished in the background, along with the wind in the trees.

And the *thing* she started seeing in the far-distant reaches of her peripheral vision?

It was no phantom Little Mum conjured by Too Much, that was for sure.

Might be . . . could be . . .

Aha!

There really *was* a cat living under the ridged-wood porch, lurking and flicking a seal-paw up through a gap to snag her unwary ankle.

Pip ventured into the garden to peer beneath the porch.

Blue eyes, slanted in challenge, met her gaze.

There really was a blue-tongued lizard in the woodpile, too, and a sly-eyed gooseberry bush down by the water tank.

Pip knew because it had bitten her. The bush, she meant . . . not the blue-tongue. Bill, as she called him, since she couldn't spell *Billardiera longifloria,* was quietly civilised — much more so than her neighbours back in Delmsford. There was that savage sentient lemon tree as well, squatting just opposite the gooseberry bush. It was old and thorny with leather-tough leaves. It bore a hearty annual crop of fruit so turgid with juice that the most delicate touch of a knife might hit one's eye with a pain that made it cry tears of outrage.

Not Pip's, however. When Pip carved into those lemons she wore swimming goggles. She'd always used them for onions, and she found them just as handy for the feral lemons.

"Ha!" she always told them as she crammed them onto the juicer.

And she imagined the sentient lemon tree shrieking *Curses! Foiled again!* accompanied by the jeers of the crafty gooseberry.

Of course she could leave the thing alone and buy her lemons at the shop, but where was the fun in that?

Her walled-in garden was a place of peace, but it was *also* a place for perils and adventures.

Pip liked the dichotomy of that.

These days, the original cat lived in the house with Pip, most of the time. She considered they were friends and companions. It was the company Little Mum's spirit had recommended.

The original cat said it wasn't so sure.

Friendship needs to be earned and worked upon. Tell no one.

Anyway, she didn't tell the back-up cat about her bucket list. Maybe she would, one day. Maybe she wouldn't.

Wise decision, the cat said. *Tell no one.*

Chapter Four. Peppery Bites

Pip didn't intend to go back to Delmsford, ever, but one day she drove two hours and a half and went to the flower show in the Delmsford Memorial Hall. It was such a 1970s occasion that she felt at home in her daisy-fronted shoes.

Entering Delmsford over the bridge felt odd. Her body braced for the rattle-bu-bump on the end of the span without help from conscious memory.

She saw the Waybridge Hotel in her peripheral vision and recalled the Saturday Suppers she used to attend when the whole Laurel-Pearmain-de-Leon family got together. Cosmo Waybridge had been the publican. She wondered if he still was.

Maybe I'll stop for supper on the way home.

But she knew she'd be long gone by then.

At the show, for the price of a two-dollar virtual ticket, she admired azaleas, marvelled at marigolds, relished the roses, pondered petunias, and wrinkled her nose at nasturtiums . . . not because she disliked them, but just to acknowledge the memory of peppery bites.

Little Nanna Pearmain used to make them into sandwiches with plenty of butter and a sprinkle of salt.

She'd have mentioned that if she'd come with a companion.

She imagined the necessary conversation she'd have had to have first. She might have gone into Jelly-and-Juice and made a casual suggestion to the lass behind the counter.

Are you going to the flower show, Wanda?

That was last week.
Not the Jellico one . . . I mean the one at Delmsford.
Delmsford.
A thoughtful silence might have ensued.
Delmsford was a country town perched on the banks of the River Delm. It was two-and-a-good-half hours away from Jellico Bay.
I'm going if you'd like a lift.
Wanda might not have wanted to commit to that long a trip with a casual though regular customer for cakes and tarts.
Better not to mention it.
Maybe old Mister Clancy might have come. She could have asked him over a cup of Indian tea and a Bushman's Best Biscuit.
Like a lift to the Delmsford Flower Show, Mister Clancy?
He'd have chewed slowly and methodically, reducing the almost impenetrable Bushman's Best to a kind of sturdy wheatmeal sludge before he swallowed and forced his front teeth through another escarpment.
Hmm?
He might be a bit deaf, but he didn't admit it.
Like to come to the flower show, Mister Clancy?
Hmm?
By the time she'd repeated it two or three times it would have seemed less than a good idea.
"You could come with me," she'd told the original cat as she jingled her car keys on their Butterfly Princess keyring.
The cat had Cat-Morsed something about *not bloody likely.*
He'd implied, with narrowed gaze, that he was a homebody and didn't care to travel.
"You must have travelled to get here in the first place. Unless you were born under the porch?"
Does that seem likely to you?
It didn't very, now she came to think of it. He seemed familiar to her, somehow, as if he might have hitchhiked in her

mind, but she couldn't place the memory he triggered.

Anyhow, he hadn't come to the show.

No one had but Pip.

While she considered nasturtiums in shades of salmon, rose, and cream, Pip hummed her mosquito queue-hum, remembering the play group that used to meet in the hall way back when in the nineties.

Apples and Pears, they'd called it. She'd gone along every Friday with Alison Blake and her small daughter, Angie.

She'd quite liked Allie, who had no relatives anywhere near, but who was emphatically not a needy soul.

She'd entirely liked the child. Angie Blake had been obsessed with the Butterfly Princess theme that used to be printed on children's clothing, school bags, and fabrics.

Pip and Angie had bonded over Butterfly Princess, because Pip had bought some shoes and a keyring from the range, and Angie had had the T-shirt and curtains. Pip's had been the grown-up version, with trailing iris wings and John Waterhouse draperies. Angie's had been pink and green, in a less sophisticated print.

Maybe Pip still had hers somewhere . . . the shoes that was. She certainly had the keyring. It pleased her far more than a generic plastic one ever could.

Sometimes, she'd minded Angie when Alison went shopping. It had never felt like an imposition and had been her idea in the first place. Angie loved stories. So did Pip. Angie was a dancing fairy child, much as Pip had been when she sat in a tree staring avidly down at the cavorting Greeks.

Pip wondered where Allie and Angie were now. Goodness! Angie would be in her twenties!

Did she still twirl to music no one else could hear?

Pip could, though generally she did use music played through her phone.

She glanced around the crowded hall, seeing the paler

circle where they'd clattered about while dancing to the *Apples and Pears* theme song. Pip used to dress up in her dancing clothes—sometimes a lilac-green tutu, and sometimes a gypsy skirt and shawl. Once she'd slipped back into a 1960s mini and platform boots and taught the children how to do the Twisty Flip.

That was so much fun, playing dancing lady with the kids. I always loved performing and they did too. Why didn't I keep on coming?

But she knew why, really. It was because Allie and Angie had moved away. One day there . . . the next day gone. Just like that.

Chad Blake might have got a transfer. Allie had said something about one being in the wind. Maybe.

Pip trilled her mosquito hum.

Maybe I could find them by doing a Find-Me search. Chad and Alison and Angela Blake.

Ring or write and say hi. Maybe invite them to visit.

Why?

They won't remember you.

Allie didn't think enough of our friendship to say goodbye.

The person ahead of her admiring the multi-toned hydrangeas raised a hand to rub at her neck beneath her Eton crop.

"Derek Blue," the person ahead of Eton Crop said. She wore a sensible pinafore in a colour Pip thought of as petrol blue.

"What about him?" Eton Crop's hand returned to hand-neutral, hanging forearm-to-hip-level.

"He's the actor who hits the most tens for me," said Pinafore, touching a supple petal with her left hand. A cloth bag printed with lavender sprigs swung forward to dangle periously close to the display.

"Don't you mean Mac Doran? Or Keith Curry?" her companion enquired.

Pip remembered them. They used to be handsome action

stars who got more press clippings than Tiny Pippin Pearmain. They were mainstream. She had never been that.

Were they still extant?

"They might make the vox-pop lists, but I have my own list." The pinafore person ahead of Eton Crop started ticking off titles on her fingers. "*Finding Moana, King Tide, Butler's Pantry*, then there's *My Bucket List*."

"I have one of those," Pip said without premeditation.

Listening in on private conversations-held-in-public was another thing she did from time to time. She reckoned it came under the umbrella of street photography law. If a conversation was held in public and in earshot of other people, then no one could blame her if she listened in.

What about taping it, though? If one can copy a scene to film or screen —

Her pondering broke off as Eton Crop and Pinafore snapped faces-right to stare at her.

Chapter Five. Cherry-Titted Nibbles and Buttered Bum

Pip, startled at their reaction to her eavesdropping and by her own voice, stared back for six seconds before recognition clanked into her brain.

Jan and Lupin. My cousins. Really? They look so old.

She was aware of a feeling of blooming warmth combined with a frisson of shock.

Family.

"Pippin Pearmain!" Lupin had recovered first. "I thought I heard a subliminal mosquito."

Jan grinned around her companion, and her late-middle-aged face suddenly rewrote itself into the gap-toothed wonder that had greeted Pip whenever she had her picture in the paper.

Tiny Pippin Pearmain as the unseen leprechaun, *as* Skipping Lilly, *as* the seventeenth fairy in *The Wishing Ring.*

Jan made an impulsive hugging motion, but apparently remembered Pip did hugs only under sufferance.

Jan let her hands drop to her sides.

"How serendipitous to see you here," Lupin put in. "Come and have afternoon tea."

Pip glanced betrayingly at the begonias, then beyond to the Potted with Panache display—did she see a begonia in a bucket?—and was it orange?—then decided she could do without begonias for another twenty minutes.

Family.

She let her cousins carry her off in their slipstream into the supper room.

"How very nineteen seventies," Lupin said, gazing at red gingham tablecloths and round-cheeked milk jugs.

They lined up at the counter, and Pip felt like jumping in a ballet leap to make sure she was seen and served.

Lupin had always been tall in an elegant-heron mode, while Jan was more the jolly hockey-sticks type—not over-weight, but brawny and without a pronounced waist.

Pip resisted the urge to tip onto her toes. It would get her maybe to chin height on the average-sized Jan.

"Cherry-titted nibbles!" Jan exclaimed with audible rap-ture as an aproned attendant advanced a "mixed plate" resid-ing on floral china for their inspection.

The aproned attendant wore the modern-day uniform of the Lilac Ladies, which boiled down to lilac binding on her apron and a tasteful *LL* monogram on the bib.

"Corned beef spread," Lupin murmured from somewhere overhead.

"Gones," Pip contributed, lapsing into family-speak.

"Mit dam-and-dream," Jan said.

"Buttered bum . . ."

"Flummery!"

Pip got up on eager tiptoe after all. "Where?"

"I was just remembering," Jan said with apology in her voice. "Big Nanna de Leon used to make it with raspberries from her garden."

"And packaged jelly, and cream from Mister Hudson's farm," Lupin recalled.

"It always smelled of summer," Jan remembered.

They sighed in unison.

"Three mixed?" the Lilac Lady prompted.

"Oh—yes." Lupin took the initiative. "And three teas . . . Pippin, do you drink proper tea these days?"

Pip skirted the question in the interests of family harmony.

"I'll drink cambric tea, since there won't be any camomile."

Lilac Lady looked puzzled.

"She means weak tea with lots of milk. It's what children in the schoolroom used to drink in the nineteenth century," Jan translated.

"Sugar's on the table," Lilac Lady said, nodding comprehension. "I'll bring your teas over in a tick."

Lupin took out a coin purse and paid for three plates and three teas in the exact amount. "Our treat, since we kidnapped you," she said as Pip slid a hand into her messenger bag and groped for her wallet.

They settled at one of the gingham-clothed tables and waited for their delivery.

No use starting a conversation yet . . . it would just be interrupted.

"So, you have a bucket list," Jan said.

Silence stretched until Pip realised Jan was talking to her.

"That is what you meant?" Lupin prompted.

"Unless you meant you, too, have a list of favourite Derek Blue films?"

That was an easy-out from Jan, who had always been kindly, but Pip didn't take it.

If she had, they might have expected her to share, and although she remembered Derek Blue as a moonlighting ex-marine in *Butler's Pantry*, she couldn't discuss his filmography with any degree of intelligence.

Derek Blue was an unlisted number, as far as she was concerned. She'd heard of him, and she'd recognise him if he entered the hall in his trademark blue singlet, but he'd never have heard of Tiny Pippin Pearmain. Whyever should he? He was mainstream.

CHAPTER SIX. LOCAL WOMAN BAKES GOOD

Pip began to hum.

"She's doing it again." Lupin rubbed her neck.

"Sorrow," responded Pip, quoting a childhood book.

"You're not." Jan pointed at her with her left hand. Her wedding ring looked comfortably established, but a wee bit dulled as if from lots of handwashing china and delving in the garden.

Pip wondered how superstitious people managed to clean their rings when they couldn't take them off. *She* had a ring that was precious to her, but it never needed cleaning because it lived in a soft little pouch in her messenger bag. She had another one, too, but that was so secret she barely remembered what it looked like. It was tucked away with her *one days* that never came.

"Why do you do that?" Lupin asked.

"Clean rings?"

"What?" Jan looked puzzled.

"*Hum*," Lupin said sternly.

"Just do. Always did."

"Just don't, then. It still makes my neck itch."

Lilac Lady brought the teas in mismatched floral cups—iris, lily, and rose.

Pip reached for the one with the rose, which looked the weakest. It wasn't quite cambric yet, so she added copious milk.

She took a sip and bit into an oozing scone.

The taste and texture were both shocking and familiar.

The Lilac Ladies who catered for the Delmsford Flower Show must still be using the *LL Gina Delmsford Hawkins Kitchen Manual*. Of course they would. The manual had been written by one of their number, back in the day, and was by far the most successful publication of LL Press.

Local Woman Bakes Good. That was what the headline must have said when it was newly published.

"Bucket list," Jan prompted, inspecting a triangular sandwich. "Egg and parsley. Yum."

She inserted the whole thing into her mouth.

Lupin took a piece of raspberry slice, then put it down. "If that's the Gina Delmsford Hawkins recipe, it'll be too sweet. I'll have . . ." Her hand hovered, and she took up a cherry jam drop.

They munched in reminiscent pleasure.

Lupin finished first. "Bucket list," she insisted, levelling her grey-eyed gaze at Pip.

Pip squirmed. Lupin was four years older than she was. She had been the senior child, tasked with watching the others at family picnics.

Tiny Pippin Pearmain might have been known as a child performer who got gifts from the studio, but that had never cut ice with Lupin de Leon.

Grown-up Lupin was the headmistress at an exclusive girls' school.

Or she had been, back in 2012.

"How are things at Mary Shelley?" Pip asked.

"Undoubtedly worse since I retired," Lupin said.

"When was that?"

"For five minutes, when she was sixty-five. Then she moonlighted for Vouch—for a driving company for a few years. Now—"

"Bucket list!" Lupin cut Jan off at the pass.

"I was just—"

"Juniper. Do I have to tell Pippin where you buried the bodies?"

Jan's jaw did an indignant drop. "You couldn't. You wouldn't."

"Try me."

"But *Lupin*—"

"We could start with *Underbloomers*."

"No!"

Jan clutched at the bib of her pinafore, which sported applique lavender and a leaping basset hound print.

It was an odd combination. Pip rather approved.

Lupin mimicked her sister with deadly accuracy, forming her elegant fingers into claws as if she was about to—

Pip felt her eyes bug.

Underbloomers? As in retro-underwear? What the hell are they talking about?

Her cousins were well into a family duel, pistols at dawn, and dam-and-dream gones were about to fly. Lupin would win the stoush because Lupin always did. She might not be more intelligent than Jan, but she had a quicker wit, and she could sometimes be cutting, which jolly tactless Jan never was.

"I do have a bucket list," Pip blurted.

Her diversion worked.

Lupin and Jan ceased hostilities, relaxed their fingers, and patted their bosoms self-consciously.

Evidently, they'd remembered they were no longer volatile children.

"Tell," Jan said. Then, with her full cheeks going pinker, she added, "Only if you want to, that is."

Pip was surprised to find that she did want to.

In her mind, the original cat disapproved.

Tell no one.

Cats don't know everything, she thought. Sometimes, one needs to share with family, and this is the only family I've got.

She had secrets — everybody did — but what harm could revealing this one do?

"You're okay — aren't you?" Jan leaned forward.

"Why wouldn't I be?" Pip asked quickly. She'd hadn't been *okay* when she flitted to Jellico Bay, but now she certainly was.

"Bucket lists are —"

"She means, she hopes you're not dying of one of those outré but ultimately boring diseases that afflict ladies of a certain age," Lupin said.

"Because bucket lists are often about getting stuff done while you still can," Jan translated.

"Of course I'm not dying," Pip said. She frowned. "Whyever would I be *dying*? I'm sixty-six."

"Oh, good. That makes —"

Again, Lupin cut Jan off. "So, what's on your bucket list, Pippin Pearmain? Elevator shoes?"

Jan jerked with indignation.

Pip waved her down. "Of course not. I don't need any. And besides, they wouldn't be buckets."

CHAPTER SEVEN. DANCING OVER SIXTY-SIX

Pip got up from the table and danced a few steps, raising her arms in a ballet curve and pointing her daisy-toed shoes.

One of the grand things about tipping over fifty . . . okay, over sixty . . . all right, over sixty-six . . . was that one no longer cared if Lilac Ladies stared.

She'd been stared at quite a lot over her lifetime, and folk had paid for the privilege.

She grinned and waggled her fingers at a wide-eyed child over at the counter with her daddy. For a moment, she was back with Angie Blake.

Yes, darling. Ladies of a certain age can dance. Don't ever let anyone try to tell you otherwise. Don't ever stop dancing, either. Dancing keeps you young and I do it every weekday morning at seven sharp, an hour before my date with juice from the sentient lemon tree.

Jan applauded silently and Lupin ate another cherry jam drop with evident relish.

They didn't care if Lilac Ladies stared either. The women of the Laurel-Pearmain-de-Leon clan never really had.

Pip gave her cousins a low court curtsy, winked at the wide-eyed child and her goggle-gazed daddy, performed a triple pirouette and resumed her seat.

"I have elevation already, courtesy of my ballet lessons," she said.

"And you still remember how after all these years," Jan

marvelled.

"Yes, of course. I do my practice every weekday morning. I am meticulous. I was never any better than average, despite my good reviews, but I reckon if I live long enough I can burst back on the scene as the dancing centenarian and make a fortune to leave to the back-up cat. Only it will be the back-up, back-up, back-up—"

"Pi to you too," Lupin said.

"And not repeating," Pip agreed. She added generously, "If you two outlive me, I can leave you some fortune too."

"Your bucket list," Lupin said. "What's on it?"

The cat in Pip's mind folded its paws.

Tell no one. Oh, I give up. Do what you will. But don't you say I didn't warn you.

Pip opened her messenger bag and withdrew the feint-lined notepad, with the green pen clipped to it.

She pushed it across the table.

Jan looked at it, looked at Pip, sighed, and took some reading glasses out of her bib pocket.

"Minutes of the meeting of the Delmsford Flower Club: January nineteenth, nineteen seventy-two," she read aloud, around the pen. "Present—good God, Pip, could you write this any smaller?"

"What fresh idiocy is this?" Lupin wondered audibly.

Pip hummed.

Lupin shot her a *look*.

"Those are old minutes," Pip admitted. She borrowed a nifty piece of syntax from Jan and made it hers. "I used to be secretary of the Flower Club here, for about five minutes, after I left school."

"Why *five* minutes?" Jan asked, having apparently not noticed Pip's appropriation of her term. "She frowned. "I don't remember that. Lu?"

"I would have been at uni that year," Lupin reminded.

"I took the job because Little Mum said I should have a fallback position and a work history if the performing didn't pan out. Only it was the job that didn't pan. They replaced me with someone who could spell *Schizanthus* and *Eschscholzia*," Pip said.

"*Dieffenbachia* and *fuchsia* always get me," Jan muttered.

"Those, too. I told them I could spell *Lupin* and *Juniper*, because they were family names, though I was shaky on Schizanthus, but they were unconvinced. Mind you, I came unstuck on *Mimulus* and *Cymbidium*. I stuck an oh in one and an ess in the other."

"Anyone might." Jan was ready with comfort, as ever.

"And yet you still come to their shows, even after being summarily sacked," Lupin marvelled.

Pip shrugged. "The sting of rejection has dissipated. It's been fifty years, after all."

"The sting of rejection never dissipates," Jan said, turning her wedding ring with a faraway gaze.

Pip didn't ask.

Instead, she explained, "The bucket list is underneath the minutes. And anyway, even if I hadn't been sacked, I'd still have had to stop being minute taker. I got a part in *The House of Heriot.*" She sighed. It would have been nice if she'd got the part in time to resign before they sacked her. It would have looked better on her employment history if she'd ever needed it.

Jan looked away from whatever she was contemplating. "I remember that film—it was a vehicle for Hope Gordon and Hein Hoffmann, but it also had that dishy actor who played the highwayman—what was his name again?"

"Alain something," Pip said disingenuously.

"That's right—Alan Balfour." Jan nodded with satisfaction at having brought the name to mind.

Unusually, for Jan, she had got it wrong, but Pip didn't bother to correct her. What was the point? It had been *decades* ago—fifty years in fact since she and Alain Barfleur had rambled the gardens of Oakengrove.

CHAPTER EIGHT. YOU WROTE A BUCKET LIST

Lupin took the pad from Jan and removed the pen with a snap. She leafed through four pages of fifty-year-old minutes and ripped them off the pad. A brisk crumple later, they landed in the industrial-sized bucket over near the counter.

Jan applauded. "You should take up netball, next. Oh—"

Lupin's hand clawed at her pearl-buttoned blouse, just missing the gold bar brooch that was her only visible adornment.

Jan cringed.

Pip's mouth formed an O of indignation but again, what was the point? Did she really think someone would come asking about Oliver White's decisions? Come to that, Oliver White was probably dead. So, most likely, were the rest of Delmsford Flower Society Committee—at least the ones *she'd* known back when she was sixteen. She hadn't seen anyone familiar bearing a badge.

Lupin had put on silver-rimmed *pince-nez*.

Really?

She was perusing Pip's green-inked bucket list with an evil grin.

She cackled.

Pip jumped. She'd forgotten Lupin's cackle. It was a mad hen sound with overtones of kookaburra abandon.

"What?" Jan made a hopeful left-hand jerk towards the

feint-ruled pad.

Lupin turned it ostentatiously out of eye-line — not that Jan could have made out any words from where she sat on the other side of the table.

"What's on it?" Jan asked.

"It's a bucket list. A literal bucket list." Lupin cackled again and skidded the feint-ruled pad over the gingham cloth.

"Careful with that — it's over fifty years old," Pip objected.

"So are we." Lupin took out a handkerchief folded like a triangular sandwich and mopped her eyes.

Jan squinted as she read the first page of the list. Her lips twitched. She smiled. "God, Pip!"

"What?"

"You wrote a bucket list."

"*Ja? Und?*"

"She's lapsing into German. That's as bad as humming," Lupin observed.

"You do it too," Jan sniped. She began to read aloud. "*One. I remember a silver bucket with a wide mouth. I think it was galvanised, but not like fogs . . . no . . . frogs. It was shiny, and Little Nanna Pearmain used it for storing swedes in the kitchen with the soil still on.*

"*Two. There was a tall white bucket, made of hard plastic with a metal handle. It held milk in Mister Hudson's dairy, and I could never lift it. I tried once, and milk slopped into my left boot. I topped up the bucket from the cold tap. I never told anyone about that. I also rinsed my boot and put it upside down over the bathroom tap to dry.*

"*Three. There was a red plastic bucket with a red handle that clicked into place. It was quite sturdy, not bendy at all, and we used to take it to the beach. It had a matching spade with a square mouth.*

"*Four. Mister Hudson told me a bull calf got his head stuck in a white milk bucket, but it wasn't the tall one. It was straight up and down, like a coffee jar, and the handle fell over the bull's poll. It was wedged, and Mister Hudson had to cut the handle off with his pliers. After that, the bucket went to Missus Hudson's garden, and she* grew mint in it. *She pointed it out to me, which is how I came to list it.*

"Five. *Little Nanna Laurel's granny used a wooden bucket to put her wet washing in on its way back from the copper. I never saw her do it, and I don't remember her at all, or even know her name, but I remember the bucket because it was in the old stable under the manger along with the copper at Nanna and Pop Laurel's place. By then it had spiders in it.*"

Jan paused. She was no longer grinning as she removed her glasses and hung them back in her bib pocket. "A literal bucket list. Why?"

Pip shrugged. "I like to do it. It's things I remember." She turned out her hands, dropping a blob of dam-and-dream off her half-consumed third gone. "Have you any idea how many buckets you can cram into sixty-six years of memories?"

"So, your bucket list isn't things you never got to do. It's things you did," Lupin clarified.

"Sort of. Only I never did buckets. I mean, I never collected them, as such."

"Only their memories."

"That's right. I like buckets. They're useful."

Jan picked up the green pen which Lupin had unclipped to facilitate tearing off the minutes. "May I?" She replaced her glasses.

Pip felt a qualm, but she had to say, "Be my guest."

CHAPTER NINE. IN THE BUCKET OF FATE

Jan turned to the first blank page and wrote for a couple of minutes. "Lupin?"

Lupin nodded and accepted the pen.

Pip wondered what buckets her cousins remembered. She looked forward to finding out. She did hope they weren't ones she knew as well.

Jan ate a final sandwich and a coconut cone while Lupin wrote on.

And on.

Jan, restoring her glasses once again to her pocket, said, "Pip, I hope you didn't mind."

"What—about the bucket list?"

"Yes. It was your secret, and we dug it out of you."

"I know, but I didn't have to share it. You two didn't hold me down and threaten to snip off my pigtails if I refused to show you."

"We never did that!"

"I never said you did. I was being metaphorical, and besides, my pigtails were insured like Hope Gordon's fingers."

Jan stared at her. "Hope Gordon had her fingers insured? How do you know? And why?"

Pip shrugged. "I think it was because she was a hand model for one of those big jewellery companies. She did glove-modelling, too, when she was younger. You know—wearing a little black dress and stretching out one hand and drawing on a glove while the voiceover said something about *timeless elegance*. I remember she said talcum powder was what they used to make the glove glide on."

"I didn't even know glove-modelling was a thing, but I can imagine it. She was beautiful," Jan said.

"Neither would I have known it was a thing if she hadn't told me. She was nice to me on-set. They all were, in that production. You know how some actors say *it was a family atmosphere on-set* in their memoirs? *House of Heriot* was just like that." She shook away some memories she didn't feel like sharing, even with family. "Anyhow, now you know about the bucket list. I'm glad."

"Why *did* you share it?"

"You're family. You remember the people I remember. You know what *gones* are, and you picked up German from Herr Fischer, just the same as I did. We know a lot of the same things, even though I haven't seen you in . . ." Her voice trailed off, as she tried to recall.

"Ten years, I think," Jan supplied. "We all met up at Aunt Rosie's funeral."

Pip nodded, dropping her gaze to her fingers, sticky with dam-and-dream and a wee bit of leaked green ink.

Jan's Aunt Rosie was Pip's Little Mum. She'd been the last of the old guard to go. The second old guard, that was. The first old guard, the three Nannas and the three Pops, had all gone off long before, in orderly procession.

"Yes. That'd be it." She wished there was a jug of hot water on the table so she could de-sticky her fingers, but Lilac Lady had served the tea directly into cups.

Oh look . . . they still have teapots with crocheted cosies.

She looked up and added, "Well . . . it's been a long while, but you've always been there in my mind. You always will be."

Jan said, "I was so surprised when you piped up from behind us. It's not as if any of us lives here anymore . . . where are you nowadays? I'm sure I should know."

Pip squirmed, but it was a direct question, so she replied,

"I'm out at Jellico Bay. I read something about the Delmsford Flower Show having its centenary and I thought I'd forgive the Flower Committee for sacking me and come along for a look. After fifty years, it was time to put it behind me."

Lupin wrote on, with the green-ink pen steadily travelling over the feint-lined page.

Jan said, "Time," in a musing voice. Then she said, "Maybe we can—"

Pip broke in, "I expect we'll catch up again right here next February. I think I'll come for the afternoon tea, at least. We can make it a new tradition and have an annual Laurel-Pearmain-de-Leon catch-up."

Jan bit her bottom lip and turned her wedding ring.

Oops. Her married name is Sharman . . . and none of us was ever a Laurel. Little Nanna was the last of us with that name, and she wasn't born that way.

"Make that a de-Leon-Pearmain-Sharman catch-up," she amended.

"Could we arrange something a bit sooner?" Jan asked, breaking in on Pip's correction.

"I'd rather leave it in the bucket of fate with a certainty for February."

That's what the original cat would advise.

To fill in the ensuing silence, Pip retreated into her head again and began to hum.

Jan got up and wandered over to talk to someone sitting at a distant table.

"I thought that was Maisie Mink," she said in explanation when she returned.

"Was it?" Pip broke her humming to ask. She turned to look at the long-ago girl who had borrowed her first plush cat and not returned the diamanté collar, but the woman in question was bending over to poke in her shopping bag.

Still feeling guilty of cat-collar-larceny after all these years? So you ought to!

"That's not Maisie Mink. That's her sister," Jan said.

"I don't think I knew she had one."

"Yes — Marguerite . . . Daisy — they're identical twins."

Pip's mind fished about for a tiny mystery just as it solved itself. "So *that's* why she kept changing her hairstyle and ducking in and out of rooms. There were two of her."

"Didn't you know?"

"No — I just thought she must be fickle when it came to her hair." *And maybe avoiding me on account of the plush cat's collar.*

"*Really*, Pippin!" Whatever else Jan might have intended to say was lost as Lupin finally finished writing and clipped the pen back to the feint-ruled pad. She got up from the table and loomed over Pip.

Pip reached for her bucket list, but Lupin said, "Sticky fingers, my girl. That deserves one hundred lines, if not a detention." She thrust the pad into Pip's messenger bag, pressing it well down into the bottom.

Pip felt the drag and pressure as the strap pulled across her heart.

"Time to go," Lupin said. "Juniper, do you have wet wipes?"

Jan took a half-used pack out of her lavender-printed bag.

Lupin indicated Pip, who felt seven years old again.

She took the wipe anyway and cleaned her sticky fingers.

Lupin appropriated it and lobbed it into the bucket near the counter. "Ha!"

Pip, with the scent of *Freshen Up* rising from her dampened hands, swallowed the last of her now-cold cambric tea. It tasted of lavender.

Jan stashed the remaining wipes in her bag. She stacked the crumby plates and slid Lupin's rejected raspberry slice into a folded napkin. "For Ron," she said.

Pip blinked.

Isn't her husband called Mark? Has she traded him in? Was that what she meant by betrayal?

Then she mentally slapped her fingers.

Ron as in Later-Ron.

Jan piled the three floral cups in a champagne totter and carried them to the counter.

Lupin waited, glancing sideways at Pip. "Goodbye, li'l Pippin," she said.

She didn't make a hugging motion. Lupin never did.

Jan came back from the counter. She turned to Pip. Her arms didn't jerk this time, but Pip raised hers slowly. "Bye, Juniper Jam Tart."

Jan went into the hug, all warm bosom and Caraway's Comforts Lavender Lotion.

It was always Jan's signature scent.

Lupin said, "If you've quite finished the hug-fest, it's past time we went."

"Bye, Loopy-Lu," Pip said. She raised her hand, thumb out.

Lupin matched her and they made a silent test of strength.

Jan said, "Pip—"

Lupin dropped her hand, conceding, with the decision still in the air. "Let's go."

Pip's cousins headed, not for the body of the hall, but towards the supper room exit onto the street.

Pip went off to examine the begonias and, by degrees, she worked her way to *Potted with Panache* where there was indeed a bucket.

It was day-glo orange, and Pip stared at it in dazed delight.

CHAPTER TEN. AREA FIFTY-TWO

When Pip got home to Lemonwood Cottage, she was somewhat tired.

She supposed driving for five hours with a couple of hours of flower-admiration and cousin-reunion in between, not to speak of the sharing of her bucket list after decades of keeping it secret — except from the original cat, who wouldn't tell anyone — was enough to make anyone tired.

"Well, except for a long-distance truckie," she caveated to the cat.

Long-distance truckies are all younger than you, Pippin Pearmain.

That was the original cat, doing Cat-Morse along with a spot of semaphore with its tail, and delivering information it shouldn't have had.

Well then.

Pip decided to pretend that proved her point.

She was still fairly full of afternoon tea, so she made herself a scratch dinner from eggs on toast.

She was fond of toast, but she rarely made it. The scent was too nostalgic.

The original cat and the back-up cat had their usual chicken and rice with home-grown veggies.

Well? The original cat looked up from its pursuit of an agile steamed pea.

Well what?

What happened to you today at the flower show, Pippin Pearmain?

"I met my cousins," Pip said. She poured herself camomile tea in her favourite cup and closed her eyes to savour the familiar vapour, unadulterated by the scent of lavender wet wipes. Her fingers traced the flowers around the curve. *Marigolds* they were, but not the stiff *tagetes*. These were the simple beauty of *calendula*.

Und? The cat could do cod German too.

"*Und* nothing. We caught up on our news and ate our afternoon tea."

Pip remembered the original cat had never met Lupin and Jan—or indeed anyone else Pip had known before her move to Jellico Bay. She told it a bit about them, to put them into context.

Were they very much changed?

The cat licked its paw. It must have given up on the pea-green survivor.

"They were. And they weren't. They were older, for one thing."

So are you. The cat's signals could be neat and precise, and sharp.

"The hierarchy is the same. Or do I mean the dynamics? Lupin is the eldest. I come next, and Jan is the youngest."

Jan. Is that the same as January? The cat whisked its tail. Pip thought it was thinking of prawns on New Year's Day.

"Jan's real name is Juniper. She changed it because she was fed up with people calling her *Junior*."

The original cat yawned, showing fine white fangs and a tongue as clean and pink as velvet corduroy.

"I'd forgotten how annoying they were," Pip added, inhaling more camomile vapour. "But I'm glad I saw them and started our new tradition. I'm glad they saw the bucket list, too."

Didn't they laugh at you?

"Yes. But they understood because they're my family."

The original cat glanced over to the other side of the room, where the back-up cat played cheerfully with a feather under a chair.

They're the same breed as you, the cat signalled. *They spring from the same old memories. Their stories are yours.*

Pip knew it was right.

Maybe I should have let Jan arrange another get-together before next year, she pondered.

Then she thought, but that would have felt intended.

And I won't look for Allie and Angie Blake on Find-Me. If they'd been at the Delmsford Flower Show today, along with my cousins, we could have played catch-up and do-you-remember. We could have parted naturally with a casual good to see you *if we weren't the way we remember one another . . .*

Not that little Angie would be the same, or even recognisable. She'd be twenty-something by now.

Maybe she has a husband or a wife, or even a couple of cats. The original cat and the back-up cat. Could even have an original dog and a back-up dog. She might not be Angie Blake anymore. Angie What? It'd be fun if she married a Laurel or a Pearmain or a de Leon . . . if there were any left to marry. But there aren't.

Pip drank her tea and washed her precious marigold cup before readying herself for the evening. She rarely used that cup because fine porcelain was so ephemeral, but today had been all about memories of the past.

TV? No. Music, maybe?

She flipped on the TV after all.

A documentary was showing on the SouthernArts channel. It was something about a winter music festival on Delphinium Island.

Where's that?

A woman played the violin—a leaping, joyous tune that was over too soon, swamped by festivalgoers with things Pip thought were called *sound-bytes*. She tuned them out in favour of wondering if anyone ever called their child Delphinium. It was a good name. It would fit in well with the Laurel-

Pearmain-de-Leons.

She switched off the TV and fetched her bucket list out of the messenger bag.

Yes. That felt right.

She unclipped the green pen and quickly turned over the used pages. Was it her imagination, or did they look some-how fatter than the ones that were still blank? Did the bucket list impart some weight, or thickness to the paper that it hadn't had before?

Page seventy should be waiting for attention, but it was al-ready occupied. That was right—Jan and Lupin had added buckets they remembered.

Family bucket. Is that a thing? Something to do with chicken.

She started to hum, focused on Jan's careful script, much bigger than her own. Jan's writing always slanted the wrong way because Jan was left-handed.

Can't write you a bucket, because I don't remember them espe-cially, except for the yellow one I keep to catch drips in the spare room when it rains.

This is a secret though.

You know I always liked reading romances and murder myster-ies? Well, now I write them. I played with "Romance is Murder" and with "Murder is Romantic" but they both just sounded creepy, so I went with "Death and Desire" as my tag. My pen name is Ju-niper Gin, and my first book is called Underbloomers. *That's a kind of pun . . . or a riddle the main characters have to solve to find the murdered bodies.*

Lupin refers to my books as bodice-rippers, as you may have no-ticed.

I really don't mind. I didn't want you to think, retrospectively, that she was being unkind.

I'm working on Book 3 now, and the setting is at a flower show. This doesn't mean I plan to off anyone down in the petunias — truly.

So now you know my secret in exchange for yours.

Xxx Jan aka Juniper Gin.

Well! And again, well! Pip felt her bucket list feint-ruled pad had drifted into Area Fifty-Two.

She supposed it was lovely of Jan to trust her with a secret, but what did she expect her to do with it?

Pip earnestly considered. Finally, she put it to the original cat.

Plain enough. She says she traded you a secret for a secret, the cat signalled. *I told you to show no one, if you recall.*

"My secret doesn't oblige anyone to do anything," Pip muttered.

Neither does Juniper Jan's.

"It does so. She's told me, and now she'll expect me to read the book, then to review it on Book-Review-Twenty-two — or something. Ring and say that I loved it, at the very least. And of course she'll feel short-changed if I don't gush into specifics."

No obligation. The cat sounded uninterested.

"She'll *expect.*"

The original cat shrugged the bony ridges of its shoulders. *Told you to show no one. Showing anyone anything leads to complications. Tell it to one who knows.*

"How do you mean?"

I showed myself to you. Now I have complications and my paws are tied.

And if that wasn't enigmatic . . .

Pip turned to page seventy-one to see what Lupin had penned.

She expected a shared memory, perhaps, told with sharp observation. She hoped it was nothing about Jan who had already been cornered into revealing her private activity by her sister's peculiar hints.

So not fair.

And how many teenaged girls had wailed that into the

silence when brought before the headmistress of Mary Shelley School for Girls?

They must have been terrified.

Pip noted Lupin had written rather a lot. Her writing was very upright, just like Lupin. Although it was written in Pip's familiar bucket-list-green pen, it managed to have angled flicks and jaunty tails as if created with a dip pen or a quill.

Pip put away penmanship envy, and the memory of that one quill pen, and started to read.

I have left it too late to start a proper bucket list, but I'm fitting in what things I can. In the circumstances, it's been more like revisiting rather than blazing fresh trails. I would like to say I had reconnecting with you on my mental agenda, Pippin, but I'm afraid the thought never surfaced. It probably wouldn't have if we hadn't chanced to meet today.

It's such a long time since we three were together, and the last several times were all to do with Baked Meats.

It's difficult to reconnect at funerals. They're full of people who feel so bad that they don't want company, and other people who feel bad because they don't feel bad – or not bad enough. Even when Juniper and I came to your mother's funeral I, at least, felt the latter sort of bad.

I am not good at feeling bad. It makes me tetchy.

When Mum arranged our dad's send-off, she bought the package deal that included her as well. That meant it was all done and dusted, and I barely needed to bestir myself beyond making the call to The Last Gift *to set the wheels turning.*

Besides, Juniper and I still had one another.

When Aunt Rosie went, you were all alone.

I'm sorry about that.

I'm sorry we didn't rally around you, but you didn't encourage rallying. You never did.

That sounds as if I'm blaming you and I'm absolutely not. I've always admired you, Pippin. You don't pretend. You go at life with an ice axe in one hand and a Butterfly Princess keyring in the other. I hope your keys have opened something nice.

So now I'd better get to the point. I hoped we'd be done with funerals, after Mum's and Aunt Rosie's. We did get a ten-year respite, apart from a few of Mum and Dad's old friends, and usually a card sufficed for their heirs and assigns. By the law of averages, we should have had a good fifteen years or so before the next Meats might need to be Baked for our diminishing clan, but it's going to be a lot sooner.

I have a few months left.

Don't ask me what a few means. Don't contact me at all. My wily, pussyfooting, Hippocratic doctors can't or won't explain. A few means two or more, but not as many as several. To me, several months thus implies five or six at least. Therefore, I expect I have more than one month but fewer than five, so we'll call it two-to-four.

As someone stated, it really focuses the mind, but I wish I had a countdown so I could throw my all into the last hurrah.

Fireworks, perhaps?

I could light a fuse. Then I'd ride off on a rocket.

In any case, modern miracles aside, I won't see another Delmsford Flower Show, and we won't eat gones and dam-and-dream again together.

I'm sorry about that.

I wish I could say I always intended to get in touch. I did, in a way, but I supposed it would happen someday, without me shoving the Ouija pointer intentionally in your direction.

It did happen that way and I'm glad to be vindicated. Serendipity, as I said.

I'm glad I saw your bucket list, too. It's a splendid mix of memories without regrets. It's so very you. So entirely Pippin Pearmain. Maybe, as well as the ice axe and the keyring, you go at life with a bucket hat on your head.

I'm not laying an obligation upon you, because I know you won't want one any more than I would. Obligations are like expensive coats that someone donates to you and which you don't feel able to toss to the charity bin.

We're quite alike, I think, you and I – more so than I am like

46

Juniper. Please, then, take this as a notion or a hope, and not as a directive or an order from beyond the grave. Indeed, I am not dead yet.

Despite what I said about the Baking of Meats, I have decided not to have a funeral. Instead, I would like you and Juniper to meet up at the Delmsford Flower Show next year. I hope you will drink tea and order three mixed plates, dance in your daisy shoes, and raise a cherry-titted nibble to me.

Perhaps you will take my ashes along, installed in an elegant bucket. You could tip me craftily into a potted plant or take me on the tour and carry me home again. On the whole, I'd prefer the latter.

Maybe you could have me for six months of the year, and Juniper for the others . . . just like Persephone after she ate the half-dozen pomegranate seeds.

This is not a directive or even a wishful hope. It's just a fanciful notion.

Lupin Coriander de Leon . . .

P.S. Did you see the bucket among the begonias? In case you didn't, it was painted day-glo orange. Tasteful.

P.P.S. I note Juniper has spilled her bodice-ripping secret in these pages. I commend Underbloomers to you. It's really rather funny.

P.P.P.S. The ellipsis after my name reflects that I'm not dead yet. None of us knows the future . . .

Chapter Eleven. Green Ink and Descant

Pip stared at her bucket list. Her world staggered as it fell off its daisy-toed shoes.

Lupin wasn't supposed to die in her sixties. Or was she seventy now? As if that made much difference.

Jan wasn't meant to be left behind, and dammit, Tiny Pippin Pearmain should not be forced into the seniority role.

She remembered telling the cat the dynamics remained the same.

But that's because I'm supposed to be in the middle of a cousin sandwich.

She stared at the green-inked lines until they blurred.

The ancient minutes were gone. Oliver White was probably dead. Jan admitted to a late-come career in bodice-ripping, and Lupin to an imminent departure and the fancy to be lodged in a bucket.

Maybe it was time to let the bucket list go.

You can't, signalled the cat, in a warm and warning purr. *Not now Jan and Lupin know it exists. Keep it up, just as you keep your dancing and your memories. The bucket list is the essence of Pippin Pearmain.*

"I will, then," Pip said. She took up the green pen, turned a page, and began on the two new buckets she'd curated that day.

She hummed as she wrote about the industrial-sized bucket near the counter in the supper room.

It used to hold ten kilos of processed pineapple. It said so in big black letters below the rim. *Lupin used it to rid me of the ancient minutes, then of a wet wipe that smelled of lavender.*

Her humming rose in pitch as she embarked on the glory of the bucket that was day-glo orange — and which held a *Potted with Panache* display of orange begonias.

Orange is such a wondrous colour. It's opposite to green on the chromatic scale . . .

She paused. "Is the chromatic scale to do with colour?" she asked the original cat.

The original cat ignored her, but the back-up cat, not-snoozing across the room, signalled diffidently in clear Cat-Morse.

Actually I believe it's something to do with music. And by the way . . . I know about the bucket list already.

"Fair enough." Pip dipped her pen in imaginary ink.

She almost heard the gentle tune of a lute as it played in the green room long ago. They'd been waiting in there for the call to do their scene — just Alain Barfleur and Tiny Pippin Pearmain. She'd wanted to dance to the music, but she'd thought it might look affected.

I wouldn't care now . . .

One day, *we said, but one day never came.*

And yet, as Lupin said, I'm not dead yet.

She considered a little more.

I'm here for you when the original cat shuffles off where good cats go, the back-up cat continued.

"Good to know someone is here for me," Pip murmured.

She put Alain Barfleur and his sweet-toned lute aside, and wrote determinedly, *Maybe that's why orange is such an unrestful sort of colour . . .*

Lost in the listing of buckets, Pip hummed happily on.

The original cat and the back-up cat began to sing a descant with their purring.

PART TWO. THE ADVENT OF LUPIN'S CAT

April 2022

CHAPTER ONE. BRAVERY

Pippin Pearmain did not consider herself brave.

She was never one of those kids who stood up to bullies or hurled herself off the top rocks at the flooded Delmsford Quarry to plunge through lime-clouded water down to the bottom where old bikes and hubcaps lurked.

There are eels in there.

Are not.

Dive down, then, and you can prove it.

Pip could swim perfectly well, but she didn't dive. It was not that she couldn't do it—more that she just didn't. There were lots of things Tiny Pippin Pearmain didn't do.

If anyone asked her why, or tried to tell her to try new things, or *why-not-come-and-have-fun,* she hummed her high mosquito trill and retreated into her mind.

She was small and odd, but bullies never bothered her at school. Cousin Lupin de Leon, Class Captain, House Prefect and later Head Girl saw to that. One glare from Lupin de Leon's cold grey eyes made bumptious boys and grasping girls find urgent business at the other end of the playground.

Pip thought Lupin's *looks* had saved a whole generation from turning to petty crime. Her eyes seemed to know exactly what one was thinking.

It was truly horrifying.

In her company, Pip felt utterly safe.

Lupin gave detentions even then. She made prohibitions, and she made suggestions, all to do with precisely why the bullies should not ever, no, *never,* even think of menacing

Juniper de Leon or Pippin Pearmain.

I shall know if you do.

The weird thing was that she did it without ever uttering a word.

Lupin de Leon was one of the world's protectors and she protected . . . whether the subject liked it or not.

Helen and Rosie, the girls' mothers, had taken note of her proclivities early on, and had laid it upon Lupin to mind her sister and her cousin. Lupin did, with a brisk efficiency that kept Juniper and Pippin in line and out of danger.

Pip thought minding the littlies was probably good practice for Lupin's later iteration as the feared and revered Headmistress at Mary Shelley School for Girls.

Other schools might go co-ed or fluid-gender. Mary Shelley never did.

Other heads might call themselves School Leaders or Principals, or *Hi, please call me Delilah. We're democratic round here.*

Lupin was emphatically a Headmistress and she stared down anyone who tried to suggest anything else. Her staff might refer to her as Headmistress, as Ma'am, or as Miss de Leon. She instilled the memo forcibly into every new teacher or support worker who joined the school. The look she gave them if they strayed from her directive ensured they thereafter remembered it, internalised it — and obeyed. Mary Shelley School for Girls was not a democracy.

Pip wondered vaguely why Lupin had never stood for parliament. She'd have fixed the nation's problems, spit-spot, if anyone had the sense to vote her in.

Whether the nation would have survived the fixing without being utterly traumatised was an interesting point to ponder.

Dealing with Lupin throughout her childhood had inured Pip to disapproval, but she didn't consider it had made her brave. It had possibly done the opposite, by taking away the necessity to struggle against adversity on her own. She had always been protected, by Lupin, by Sully, by Little Mum and Little Dad, by the Nannas and the Pops . . . until she wasn't.

She knew she wasn't adventurous by nature, either.

Even in her hormonal teens she didn't hanker to bestride a motorcycle, or to join a fast man — or a fast woman for that matter — to go fishtailing in a kamikaze car with flame decals painted along the sides and giant spoilers.

She had no truck with strange substances, whether swallowed, inhaled or, lord save her, injected. Camomile tea and aspirin were as pharmaceutically daring as she ventured.

Risks were something other people took while Pip looked on with mild wonder that they should bother.

She knew the desire for taking risks was something to do with the chemical balance in one's brain. There had been studies done with adolescent rats. She also knew some people had something called adrenaline rushes associated with courting danger. She'd never had one of those and she didn't want one.

By now, in the autumn of 2022, secure in Lemonwood Cottage with the cats for company, she assumed she never would.

CHAPTER TWO. ON BEING SMALL

Tipping over the hill of sixty-six with a height of just under 150 cm and a weight of 40 kg after a large meal might have bothered some women, but it didn't trouble Pip. She'd always been small and frail-looking, but on the whole it had worked in her favour.

Pip and her agent, Sully, made sure of that.

Her wavy, baby-soft, waist-length hair, hazel eyes, and delicate wrists and ankles made her look like a winsome sprite, and someone who needed to be cared for. Pip let it happen . . . until she decided she'd had enough.

At that point, the startled person carrying her bag of books, mending her puncture, paying for her coffee or fixing her front fence would find himself—it generally was a *he*—thanked with a bland smile while Pip's suddenly steely eyes suggested he ought to be *on yer bike, make like a tree,* or *run along, dearie.* It usually worked.

She was also good at being vague, never quite agreeing to things other people thought were a foregone conclusion.

Maybe, could be, let's see, and *possibly* were favoured words in Pippin's lexicon.

Being small, winsome, and sprite-like had bought her a whole career, if one discounted talent.

Would I have had as much success, or any, if I hadn't been Tiny Pippin Pearmain?

She'd never asked that of anyone but herself, but she feared she knew the answer.

Of course I wouldn't. Who wants another actor who looks the same as the last nineteen who auditioned? Who needs another wide-mouthed beauty on racehorse legs? Who needs another curvaceous kiss-lipped blonde?

It was her size and her general feyness that had brought the roles to her . . . along with Sully.

Sully seemed to know when a role for Pip was in the offing . . . possibly even before the scriptwriter did.

Pip suspected she sometimes planted the idea of those roles, perhaps with the aid of a foaming mug of Fagus ale.

Roles begat roles in eccentric zig-zag progression.

And now I can be the dancing centenarian and make a new fortune — that's if I live that long.

That caveat was a new one, born on the day of the Delmsford Flower Show, in February.

CHAPTER THREE. THE FLIT

2012

No one offered help when Pip sold her mother's house and her glorious garden and moved to Jellico Bay in 2012. Pip neither wanted nor needed any assistance or advice, so she didn't give anyone the chance. She informed no one but the real estate agent of her intentions until the deal was done. It had been Too Much, but talking about it would have made it worse.

She supposed and hoped that by the time the Delmsford locals noticed she'd gone, her redirected mail, cancelled newspaper, and lack of delivery orders from the Delmsford Community Supermarket would have taken effect.

Pippin Pearmain had effectively flitted from *Treasures*, the house she'd inhabited for fifty-something years, and settled like a homing pigeon in an old but convenient cottage near the sea.

Lemonwood, it was called, and it simmered gently behind its high drystone wall. She couldn't remember why she'd chosen Jellico Bay as her new home, unless—yes! That was it! She'd once spent an enchanted week there with Big Nanna de Leon and Jan and Lupin. They'd gone to a café—might have been Jelly-and-Juice if it had existed back then—and Pip, ever restless, had gone for a walk on the beach.

She'd been enjoying the sunshine, and half-watching wheeling gulls when a distant glint caught her eye. She'd wandered over and stubbed suspiciously at the glint with her shoe. Sea glass? Pip liked sea glass. She picked the thing up and put it in her pocket . . .

She still had it, and it wasn't until she'd moved to the bay for good that she learned how lucky she'd been to find a Jellico diamond. People looked for them all the time. Some, like Pip, picked one up on a casual stroll, while others might hunt assiduously for weeks without seeing one. There were all kinds of theories about the best time to find one . . . after a storm, when the crabs were on the move, or, according to some, while walking backwards, naked, in the first light of a full moon.

It was probably the memory of that piece of luck that drew her to the bay. It was another piece of luck that Lemonwood Cottage was vacant just when she needed a home.

She didn't mention her relocation to anyone—not even to her de Leon cousins, who were the only family of the blood she had left after the passing of Little Mum Rosie.

Long-ago friends had shown her how effective a flit could be.

1997

Alison Blake and her small daughter Angie had been good company, but then, abruptly, they'd moved without leaving a forwarding address.

It had taken a few days for Pip to notice. She recalled dressing up in her gypsy dancing clothes for their weekly session at the Apples and Pears playgroup.

She recalled pondering whether or not to make any camomile tea while she waited for Angie's happy hailing from the porch. It would get cold if they came to fetch her on time, but it could be reheated.

She'd made some anyway and drunk it . . . and she'd suddenly realised the playgroup had started an hour ago and

Allie and Angie still hadn't come to fetch her.

What? Was it a public holiday? Could Angie be ill with whatever was going around? Had they expected her to walk to their place to meet them? Why would they think she'd do that? It wasn't their standing arrangement. *Treasures*, where she still lived with Little Mum and Little Dad, was closer to the hall than the sixties bungalow where Angie lived with her parents. *Treasures* was on their way.

And they *did* have a standing arrangement. It was one of the very few unbreakable and certain arrangements she made.

She might be shifty and insubstantial when some folk tried to pin her down, but she'd *never* disappoint Angie.

If she was in Delmsford on a Friday, and not at work, she went to Apples and Pears to dance with the children. Sometimes Angie walked back home with Pip, and they spent a happy hour or so together while Allie shopped for groceries or . . . well, did whatever Allie did in her child-free time.

Pip didn't call Allie that day, in case there was an emergency or a mistake, but three days later, she walked around to their house. Her ostensible reason, barring emergencies, was to admire Angie's new pink Butterfly Princess bed, but her visit was really to find out what had gone amiss.

When she arrived, the place had that blank-eyed look that suggested it had never heard of the people she'd come to see, and that probably they'd never existed.

Pip circled the garden. The petunias she'd helped Angie to plant were just coming into flower with shocking purples and pinks and the occasionally frilly ballet-dress white.

A stray plastic bucket, once red, but now sun-bleached with just a few pink veins in its cracks leaned drunkenly under the clothesline, half propped on a piece of brick.

Angie had evidently been using it for her crayon collection.

The child was always drawing when she wasn't listening

to stories or coaxing Pip to dance.

Pip considered the broken crayons with their peeling wrappers and left them be. They weren't hers, and neither was the bucket, which had seen much better days.

She did add a detailed description of the bucket to her bucket list. It was a handy method of appropriation without active theft. Pip was a fan of such interesting dichotomies.

She was *not* a fan of being dropped without a by-your-leave — and the pain of it stung for weeks.

She missed Angie with her lively chatter.

Little Mum and Little Dad talked to her, but their conversations were domestic and general. When Little Mum and Aunt Helen got together they often lapsed into twin-speak, leaving Little Dad and Uncle Lance de Leon to talk about cabbages and kings.

Pip found Angie's conversation always entertaining. Angie was intrepid but she also had good sense.

CHAPTER FOUR. STILL YOUNG

1997

Pip's bucket list was nothing like anyone else's, being a literal list of buckets.

When she realised her young friends were never coming back, Pip packed away her dancing clothes and found something else to do on Friday afternoons when she didn't have to work.

Little Mum Rosie must have noticed the change in Pip's routine, but she never said anything. Little Mum and Pip understood one another. They both liked camomile tea and they valued silence. Little Dad patted her shoulder one evening and offered her a box of Caraway's Comfits.

Pip accepted and sucked the spicy sweetness to soften her hurt.

1964

Right back in the early 1960s, Little Mum had arranged for the Sullivan Gilbert Agency to manage Pip's affairs.

"It will save trouble," Little Mum said serenely.

She didn't say whose trouble she meant, and Pip never asked. It just *was*. Little Mum arranged it, and so it was right and good. Little Nanna Laurel approved. It might even have been Little Nanna's idea. It was difficult to say. Sometimes, what the small ladies of the Laurel-Pearmain-de-Leon clan wanted merged into a self-perpetuating event—a joint idea.

Big Nanna de Leon could not be called small by any degree, but she generally wanted the same thing as the others. If it was good for the family, that was good enough for Big Nanna.

Sullivan Gilbert — who was a lady in spite of her name — was good for the family.

She liked the asset and she understood how best to utilise an asset — the asset being Tiny Pippin Pearmain.

Win-win-win was Sullivan Gilbert's mantra. It boiled down to Send the asset for the best roles, train the asset to work hard and well, and ensure the asset is treated with scrupulous fairness. Threaten the bollocks of anyone who attempts to sidestep directive three and, if necessary, be prepared to carry through on that threat.

Pip had loved and respected Sullivan Gilbert.

"Luv, if any man — or woman — tries anything you don't think is to your benefit, holler out *now*. Don't ever keep quiet if a hand goes where it shouldn't. Holler *now*, holler *loud*, and Sully will get out her nutcrackers."

Sullivan Gilbert often referred to herself in the third person. Pip found it comforting. It gave her a mythic status.

After all these years, Pip understood herself almost as well as she'd understood Little Mum and Sully.

She was stung and annoyed, but she refused to grieve — much — for the loss of a friendship with the A-gals when they flitted.

If they'd cared at all about me they'd have let me know they were going and kept in touch — Allie could have, anyway.

On deeper thought, she utterly absolved Angie. A child of four or five had little autonomy. She couldn't even choose to accept a gift if her mother forbade it.

If Allie had cared even a bit . . .

Later, in 2012, that thought came back to bite her.

At the time, she simply accepted Little Dad's offer of a box of Caraway's Comfits and found something else to do with her Fridays.

The Blake Family Flit had happened nearly a quarter of a century ago. Pip supposed she must have been forty-something then—at that age where people might say, bracingly, "You're still young," while suggesting, in subtle subtext, that it was time to get cracking with certain activities and probably too late to be thinking of others.

It was but a tiny step from "You're still young," to "You're not getting any younger," and another to "If you don't do it soon it will be too late."

By the time it really was too late, Pip was somewhat glad. In her mid-forties, no one could possibly suggest she ought to get cracking on any new and uncharted activity, such as marriage. She wasn't getting cracking on anything until her knees did, and so far, they didn't. Two decades later, they still hadn't.

Pip credited her daily ballet practice and her weekly strawberries and cream with keeping those knees nicely oiled.

Long walks along the beach to the Jellico Rocks, seeking the elusive crystals called *Jellico diamonds,* must help as well.

Sometimes, she stopped at the Jellico Historical Society rooms to study their potted histories. She was trying to find out the provenance of Lemonwood Cottage, but even after a decade she'd had little luck from there.

Old Mister Clancy, her neighbour, said he'd heard the first owner was called Richaud Citron and that he'd built the cottage after he retired from the sea.

"My feral lemon tree can't be that old, surely?"

Mister Clancy shrugged and said he didn't know. "You could judge the age by cutting it down and counting tree rings."

Pip shuddered at the idea. The sentient lemon would *not* react kindly to being murdered. It would probably creep into the cottage at night and haunt her dreams.

Since Mister Clancy knew more than the Historical Society

seemed to, she asked him about the name of the town itself.

"Named after Citron's ship . . . *Jellico*," he said. He sipped his powerful brew of Indian tea before he added, "The old name of the place was Baydetrorsha."

"Bay de what?"

"Baydetrorsha." He spelled it out. "Mind, that's a phonetic rendering of the even older name."

"Ja. *Und*?"

"*Baie des trois chats*," he said with a creaky chuckle. He added, "*Pouvez-vous parler Français*?"

"*Non.*"

"But you do *Deutsch sprechen*?"

"*Nein.* Just picked up a bit from a family friend. What does Baydetrorsha mean?"

"Bay of the three cats," he said, pushing his plate across for another biscuit.

"Why?"

"Chats means—"

"No, why the name?"

He shrugged. "Who knows? Maybe someone saw three cats there or had three cats . . . or maybe there were three women named Catharine, or three old ladies. Could be any number of reasons."

Pip nodded thoughtfully and sipped her camomile tea. She offered Mister Clancy a Caraway's Comfit, but he bit into a Bushman's Best Biscuit instead. She saw the hard flex of his jaw as he levered the impenetrable hard tack.

"You know such a lot," she said respectfully.

He tapped the side of his head and chewed the bite he'd taken.

"Knowing's like eating these things," he said, rapping the rest of the Bushman's Best on the edge of Pip's table. "It's hard won, and not always digestible, and after you get some you sometimes wonder why you bothered."

He took another bite, see-sawing the biscuit energetically to gain some traction.

"On the other hand, it keeps you striving," he said through a mouthful. "And once you stop striving, my dear Miss Pearmain, you die."

CHAPTER FIVE. NAMING THE CATS

2022

On an April day, Pip was working on her bucket list in Lemonwood Cottage at the edge of Jellico Bay. The original cat, whose name she had lately divined to be Kittisack, purred approval at her feet.

Kittisack looked like a seal point Siamese, but Pip was sure he was secretly something else.

Seal points were exotic and oriental, but they were still normal cats. Surely, normal cats didn't communicate in Cat-Morse?

Kittisack did.

When Cat-Morsing began, Pip had briefly considered betaking herself for a mental health assessment or, at the very least, for a check-up. She'd tossed the idea away. She felt all right. She didn't believe she was Cleopatra, Marie Antoinette, or Anna Pavlova. She was quite secure in being Pippin Pearmain. She didn't mutter to herself in queues, or wear tinfoil beanies in winter. She never carried a bent coat hanger to deflect the alien rays, although she used one occasionally for fishing for things she'd managed to drop through grates.

Nothing much had changed in the essence of Pippin Pearmain, so she concluded Cat-Morse probably was a phenomenon—real but largely undescribed.

The original cat's messages were oblique, and occasionally insightful. He might have been a spymaster in another life.

The second cat, the back-up, was a gentle calico queen

whose name appeared to be Amberjill. She was not much more than a yearling, and Pip thought she was probably Kittisack's apprentice. She'd never caught them mentoring or being mentored, and they generally seemed to live separate lives. It must be part of the plan.

"What is the plan?" she asked Kittisack as he groomed his cream belly and spat out a tuft of fur.

Kittisack glanced at her with tilted blue eyes and rededicated himself to his toilette.

Amberjill chased a leaf across the porch. She was as light as a breeze, a definite autumn spirit.

Pip thought she might be fond of her if she could only pin her down for more than five minutes.

"The plan?" she repeated without much hope.

Kitchens must always contain cheese, the original cat stated. He began on a raised hind leg. *Tell no one.*

Chapter Six. The Clancy Bucket

Pip gave up on the plan—for now. Kittisack wanted cheese. What else was new?

She returned to describing a bucket she'd purchased at a local deceased-estate auction the day before.

Old Mister Clancy had stopped striving.

That was what Pip supposed must have happened.

At any rate, he was gone.

They'd drunk a lot of tea together—his strong Indian and her camomile. Besides snips of history of Jellico Bay, they'd discussed bees and marigolds, the relative worth of Jellico diamonds, dolphins, Caraway's Comfits, which she liked and he didn't, and the many uses of eucalyptus oil.

In their decade of friendship, they had never ventured into personal territory. Pip had no idea whether there had ever been a Missus Clancy, and she'd never ask. If he knew she was Tiny Pippin Pearmain, the former darling of the alternative indie film set, he never mentioned it.

When he'd died quite suddenly and without acknowledged heirs, his estate was sold up, and Pip, as she'd promised him and herself a year before, bought his hand-carved wishing well and its attendant bucket to install in her garden.

He'd liked the idea of her having them one day, and so did she.

He'd said in his deadpan voice, "I'd will them to you, Miss Pearmain, but I want to leave something substantial to charity."

"What charity?" Pip had had to repeat it a couple of times

before he'd answer. Perhaps it was personal, but she needed to know. If it was something she couldn't approve of she wouldn't enrich it, even to obtain such a superior bucket.

"Soul-Cushion," Mister Clancy had admitted finally. "Gives kids with soul-cold a cushion while they get themselves together."

Pip had heard of soul-cold. It came into a story in her favourite book in the world. *Grandmother's Sunshine* had belonged to Little Nanna Pearmain, then to Mum. Now it was hers.

She approved of that charity, and she thought Little Mum would have, too, so she went to the sale and bought the wishing well and the bucket.

She also attended his funeral, where she'd finally learned his first name—Donovan—and his age—a good ten years more than she'd expected.

No wonder he'd stopped striving.

There was a time and a place for everything to end.

The priest, a man she didn't know, was tall and elderly, with red hair going grey. He couldn't have been Catholic, because he had a twinkly eyed wife who poured the tea at the tiny get-together in the community church hall. They'd been accompanied by another woman, tall and wearing her hair in a long tawny braid, who might have been their daughter, although she didn't look like either of them.

Pip, who usually kept herself to herself, had been surprised by a desire to introduce herself and *make friends*, as Little Mum might have put it. They looked like her sort of people, but she hadn't approached them for more than a courteous murmur of thanks for their support. They weren't locals, so what would have been the point?

Now she rather wished she had been more friendly. They might have told her things about Mister Clancy that would help her to interpret him. He'd had such an interesting mind.

The Clancy bucket was made of strips of wood, held together with metal bands like a barrel. It was old. The bolts or nails — Pip was unsure which they were — were possibly brass, but they'd gone as dark as molasses over their seventy or so years of existence. The wood was rich and glossy with the oil Donovan Clancy used to keep the cracks at bay. He'd left the recipe for his bucket oil inside the wishing well, thoughtfully addressed to new owner — Miss Pippin Pearmain.

Pip loved that bucket. It was special. It reminded her of Indian tea and Bushman's Best Biscuits, interesting conversations, and of course, of Mister Clancy. She wished he hadn't died, but since he'd stopped striving, it must have been his choice in a way.

She was sure he'd faced that next inevitable step with the same placid certainty and determination he'd shown with the Bushman's Best.

She pictured him stepping over the threshold, wearing his green rubber boots, folding his arms and lifting his chin.

"*Tá. Agus?*" That, he'd told her was what her favourite cod German comment translated to in the language he'd learned from his grandad long ago.

She hoped whoever was in charge would give him a spade and show him somewhere to dig up the turf for a garden.

Usually, she numbered her bucket list selections with a plain digit followed by a full stop, but she felt her new treasure deserved something more.

She'd seen a calligraphy font called *The Cat's Whiskers* online, so she looked it up and carefully traced the appropriate figures with her green pen.

Pleased with the effect — calligraphy in miniature — she went on with her description.

CHAPTER SEVEN. YOU MISSED A CALL

Pip had just about finished writing up her new bucket when her phone gave a muffled trill from the messenger bag where she'd left it.

What?

It always startled Pip these days when her phone rang, because it so seldom did. Most calls were from people who had no business and no right to call her anyway. Pip used to hang up on them, but old man Clancy had taught her a better way. Nowadays, as soon as she was sure it wasn't someone who deserved a hearing, she laid the phone gently aside and went out into the garden. It amused her to check the log later to find out how long they'd stayed on the line, haranguing empty air.

Probably, it saved some other poor soul from being interrupted by calls that were annoying at best and criminally-intended at worst.

How do they dare?

Pip never considered herself a particularly good person, but she'd be damned if she'd ever telephone a stranger with the intention of doing them harm.

Annoying people who deserve it doesn't count.

Better answer that, the original cat signalled from down by her feet.

When Pip didn't make an immediate move, he stuck his claws in her ankle, just hard enough to make the back of her neck prickle.

Is that the way Lupin feels when I hum? she pondered, rubbing at her neck.

The phone rang five more times before it cut out.

Pip relaxed.

Her ankle stung as Kittisack flexed his claws.

The phone chirped, announcing she had missed a call.

"And did not leave a message," Pip quoted smugly aloud.

They never did, those wretched wicked callers.

Ping!

"Okay—and did leave a message."

Maybe it wasn't a creep after all.

Could be a survey, or a call from Jelly-and-Juice about her order from Queen of Tarts.

It can wait.

Chapter Eight. Camomile Tea

Pip wrapped up her loving description of the Clancy bucket with a green full stop. She clipped her pen back onto the feint-lined notepad and glanced at the messenger bag on the kitchen counter.

It's probably time for a cuppa anyway. I'll raise my marigold cup to good old Mister Clancy.

Curiosity warred with reluctance.

If it's important, whoever-it-is will ring back.

She got up, paused to let the cat disentangle his claws from her green tights, and went to put the kettle on.

She made the tea, humming, and spread butter on two Bushman's Best Biscuits. She'd bought a five-pack on special at the Jellico Bay Essentials supermarket back in early March, but they'd broached only the first pack when Mister Clancy stopped striving.

I'll miss him a lot.

The thought startled her.

She'd never thought of them as being close friends, but now she knew they had been.

I hope the priest was right when he said Donovan had gone to his reward. I hope he has a garden with hives of bees and buckets of honey. I hope he's digging sods over right this minute.

The phone pinged a resentful reminder.

Look at it right now, Kittisack signalled in staccato Cat-Morse.

"Do I have to?" Pip whined.

Just do it.

"Now you sound like a life coach."

Pip sipped the tea, burned her lip, and concluded it served her right for procrastinating. Whenever she did something wilfully wrong, she paid some tiny forfeit to the universe.

She put down her marigold cup with care. Not for anything would she let it break, but who know when the universe might decide otherwise?

She slipped her hand into the messenger bag and extracted the phone. It was a Mark One Pink Princess — the second one she'd had. Its acquisition represented one of her triumphs against the universe. The universe wanted her to have something modern.

This is our most popular model, the universe enticed, proffering something chrome and covered with icons.

Ja. Und?

It has the following features.

But I want another Pink Princess.

She had prevailed.

You missed a call . . .

"I know that you idiot," she said to the phone. "Your Highness," she added, out of respect for its rank.

It was probably a dowager princess, or a senior princess or something like that by now.

She opened the message folder, fumbling a bit because she so rarely got a message she wanted to read.

The number was unfamiliar. That wasn't surprising.

The message that bloomed onto the screen was unsigned, but Pip knew who it was from — who it *had* to be from — because there was no one else who could have written it.

She read the six words three times over, waiting for them to sink into her consciousness.

Six tears flowed down her cheeks to make room for the words.

CHAPTER NINE. RESHUFFLING THE PACK

Cabinet reshuffles seemed to happen often, according to the news. Packs of cards were shuffled and reshuffled many times during the period of a game.

Patterns shuffled and reformed in the tin kaleidoscope Pip had loved as a child. She'd given that to little Angie Blake. Maybe it should have gone to Juniper's girl, but she hadn't thought of it.

Pip had tried to fit herself and her cousins into a virtual pack of cards, but it didn't work. There were three of them. They might be three Queens, but which ones? Who was missing?

Maybe Juniper, who called herself Jan, could be Queen of Hearts, since she was kind, generous, and warm-hearted. Imperious Lupin might be Queen of Spades since spades represented the warrior class. Lupin fought a doughty battle when she chose, and she always won. But where did Pip herself fit? Diamonds implied wealth, and clubs, hard work. Neither of those was a comfortable niche for Pip. She had enough money to see her through, and she worked hard when she had a part. Lately that hadn't applied.

You know perfectly well you're the Joker — the wild card, the original cat signalled.

He licked his claws, possibly removing infinitesimal threads of Pip's green tights, or even microscopic pieces of Pip.

"What do cats like you know about cards?" Pip asked, wiping her cheeks with the backs of her hands. Her voice sounded a wee bit choked and she swallowed the lump in her throat.

Oh, we know a lot about many things. It's our business to know about things.

"I need to reshuffle myself. I used to be safe in the middle of the pack, but now I'm exposed at the top. I'm a Swedish smorgasbord instead of a proper Australian sandwich. I feel . . . old."

How do you think I feel, Pippin Pearmain? Kittisack sniped.

Pip avoided that with a neat mental sidestep. She knew the original cat was at least eleven. He'd come with the cottage, and he hadn't been a kitten when she moved to Jellico Bay back in 2012.

How long do cats live anyhow?

We live until we've finished the business of living, the original cat responded. *Then, we stop striving and go where good cats go.*

I didn't say that aloud.

The cat chuckled. *You didn't have to. I can read your miiiind.*

His whiskers twingled and he managed to imbue that last word with a ululating wail.

The back of Pip's neck prickled in earnest.

She tried a different tack. "How can I put my heart back together? I think it just broke."

That's easy, Kittisack said.

Amberjill floated in from the porch and leaped into Pip's lap. She ducked under the edge of the counter where Pip had sat down with her now-blank phone. She gazed into Pip's eyes, in a rare display of affection.

You can't, she signalled.

"But—" Pip stared until the back-up cat's compassionate autumn eyes swam in her vision.

You can't because you shouldn't. You can't mend a broken heart. You have to wait for it to heal itself. It will do that, if you let it.

"Queen Victoria's heart never got over Albert."

If you let *it,* Amberjill reinforced.

That made sense, Pip supposed.

She woke her phone and eyed the message again through watering eyes.

Pippin – Lupin died peacefully this morning.

It was from Jan, obviously.

There was no one else it could possibly have been from.

Jan had a husband — Mark — and that grown-up daughter, but Pip barely remembered them. To her shame, she couldn't even recall the daughter's name. She remembered her as a cheerful freckle-faced kid who played sport. At twelve, she'd already been bigger than Pip. *Michaela . . . Widmark, Clark* — surely not — that was Superman. *Clarkia.* That was it! *Clarkia Sharman.* She remembered Lupin saying how clever Jan thought she was to come up with a plant name, to satisfy the tiny Laurel-de-Leon-Pearmain family requirements, while still riffing off her husband's name in a rhyming fashion, to mollify him that he hadn't got a son who might have been a complete namesake. To do him justice, Mark was a good dad, as far as Pip knew. She distinctly remembered him driving Clarkia to one of her endless soccer matches. Or was it cricket? Badminton, even?

Pip tried to picture the uniform. Surely, it had included a stick of some sort.

Hockey. That was it. Clarkia played hockey.

Mark was a blokey bloke, in low-slung jeans and a flannel-ette button-down shirt.

Lupin.

Well, they'd known it was coming.

Chapter Ten. She *Looked* All Right

L upin had written of her upcoming fate in Pip's bucket list notepad when they'd met at Delmsford Flower Show back in February. She'd said not to contact her, and Pip had acceded to her wishes. That had been easy, since in this case, Lupin's wishes aligned with Pip's.

Lupin had interpolated from her doctors' hedged-about words that she had fewer than four months left.

Obviously, she'd been right. Two months were what she'd got, almost to the day since they'd met at the flower show.

"I'm glad. She wouldn't have wanted to linger."

Are you sure? Kittisack asked.

"Well, *I* wouldn't. When it's time to go, I don't want to sit about waiting. I'd want to go midway through a packet of biscuits, like Mister Clancy. He ate one on the Tuesday, but when he came on Friday he said he'd like a Shamrock tart instead. *Easier to eat,* he said. He gave up striving."

Kittisack gave her a long, unblinking look.

"Okay, so I'm not Lupin or Mister Clancy. And I have no idea what was wrong with Lupin, anyway. She didn't write that down. She *looked* all right."

She thought back, wincingly, to that meeting in February.

Her first impression had been that Lupin and Jan looked older than they should. Then she'd had to acknowledge the decade since they'd last met — or even been in contact. Of *course* they looked older. So did she. Aside from that, they'd looked the way she should have expected. Jan was stalwart, yet cosy in a petrol-blue pinafore with lavender sprigs and a basset hound appliqued to the bib. Her outdoorsy skin was slightly tanned, and her nails were clipped short for domestic work, but the lines of her face were kind.

Lupin had her iron-grey hair in an Eton crop, and she wore heeled court shoes with a sensible navy skirt and pearl-buttoned blouse. Her skin had looked younger than Jan's, but that was because she adhered as firmly to her Caraway's Comfort Kissed by Dew moisturising ritual as Pip did to her ballet practice and weekly therapeutic dose of strawberries and cream.

Lupin had not looked ill. She had looked like Lupin, only older.

I would have noticed if she'd looked ill.

At least, she hoped she would.

She ate plenty of cherry-titted nibbles.

"I suppose I ought to phone Jan back," she said.

She hoped the original cat would give his usual advice, which boiled down to *tell no one*, or *do nothing*, but the cat signalled that yes, she should make the call.

I told you to answer that phone.

Pip said, "I will then—after I make up a batch of oil for the Clancy bucket."

Kittisack got up and swaggered out of the room with his tail swinging in counterpoint to his spine.

How do cats do that? And why do cats' bottoms manage to look so accusing?

Pip looked down at Amberjill in her lap.

The back-up cat avoided her eye, slid down under the counter, and headed for the porch to re-engage with her blowing leaf.

Some help you are.

Pip felt their disapproval. It didn't bother her—much. She'd been disapproved of by experts.

Only when she was on stage, in plays or ballet lines, or floating through film in quirky soft-focus roles, did folk wholeheartedly approve of her.

Sully said she had magic in her aura.

Not all newspaper reviews mentioned her, but the ones that did called her *Tiny Pippin Pearmain* and tried to distil her delightful stage and screen persona into words.

Now and again, Pip turned on the television in the afternoon and caught a phantom glimpse of herself in one of her early on-screen roles . . . sometimes it was just the credits.

And Pippin Pearmain as Arabella Junket.

She'd liked being Arabella, who bounced around the main characters like a wisp of . . . something or other.

Pippin Pearmain as Dream Child.

Dream Child had been fun as well. She'd been there but not there in the surreal film of the same name. Despite the title, the film hadn't been *about* Pip's character. Dream Child had been a catalyst, a snare, a reward and an illusion.

Prompted by the sting of her lip where she'd scalded it with camomile tea, she hit the telephone icon on her Pink Princess phone to return Jan's call.

I expect she's already on the phone to someone else. She won't answer. We'll play message-ping-pong all day.

How did she get my number?

CHAPTER ELEVEN. NO BAKED MEATS

Jan answered the phone on the second ring. "Pippin?"

"How did you get my number?"

"You called me." Jan sounded perplexed.

"I'm returning your call."

"Oh. Yes. Sorry, Pip. I should have called before and kept you updated."

Pip paused to try to unscramble that. Jan hadn't answered her question, but she didn't like to persist. Jan was clearly off-balance and might sob at any minute.

She drew a deep breath. "Juniper Jam Tart, I'm so sorry." She let her voice be warm, but not *too* warm. She was honestly sad for Jan and for her own snapped heart, but what was it that Lupin had said? Something about the right to sadness at funerals . . . Pippin Pearmain was a cousin, who had been AWOL from the remnants of her family for a decade, and she had no right to be as sad as Jan, who was a sister and who had presumably stayed in touch.

Jan sniffled. "So am I."

Pip said reluctantly, "Would you like me to come to you? I'd be happy to help with any arrangements."

"I don't need help." Jan's distant voice sounded breathy, as if she'd been crying a lot already. Fair enough. She had a right to many more than Pip's six tears.

Jan went on, "That sounds ungracious, but it's true. I *don't*. There's nothing much to deal with. Lupin made arrangements with *The Last Gift* – the way Mum did, remember?"

Pip remembered Lupin had told her that too.

Aunt Helen had died six weeks before Little Mum.

Little Mum had *not* stopped striving. She'd been looking at a tulip catalogue the day she died.

Maybe, Pip concluded, life just ran out for some people, interrupting them in the middle of what they were doing.

Little Mum had been sad and diminished at the loss of her sister. She had *not* stopped striving.

Still got you, Pipsy-pola.

I know, Little Mum. We've still got one another.

Jan went on, "I should have rung you and told you that Lupin was sick, but she didn't want me to. You know her — she never likes — liked — a fuss."

Not unless she was the one making it. Holy hell, could Lupin de Leon make a fuss if she chose!

Often it was a silent fuss, which made it all the more formidable.

"I did know she wasn't well," Pip admitted.

"You —"

"Remember how you wrote a secret in my bucket list about being Juniper Gin and writing novels? Lupin wrote something too. She told me she was ill — no details — and she said not to contact her, and so I didn't."

Jan whooshed out a sigh. "Then it's not a shock to you."

"It is, actually. Not nearly as bad as for you, obviously. I do hope —"

"We were expecting to have more time. It was sudden in the end, but she was prepared. She left me a letter, telling me about the arrangements she'd made. *No Baked Meats,* she said."

Pip ventured, "Did she mention you and me meeting up at the next flower show to remember her?"

"Yes! And she asked me to obtain her a dedicated bucket, and to make sure it's a jolly good one. She said *you*'d know what she meant. Do you?"

"I do."

"Will you do the honours?"

"Yes! I have the perfect one." Pip told her cousin about the Clancy bucket. The tightness behind her eyes eased.

Jan knew about the bucket list. It felt good to share that secret. Pip couldn't hug Jan, or help her with Baked Meats, but she could and would provide a magnificent bucket for Lupin's final repose.

Chapter Twelve. A Safe Ten Months Away

"Sounds like a plan." Jan seemed more like herself already. "I'll call you before the flower show," Pip promised. The next Delmsford Flower Show was a safe ten months away.

"A bit sooner . . . I'll need the bucket well before then."

"Yes . . . yes. I suppose you will. I'll—"

"I'll come to visit, and you can give it to me then," Jan said.

Cornered, Pip said, "I could come to you and drop it off."

"No . . . I'll be glad to get away. You're at Jellico Bay, right? I've never been back since that holiday with Big Nanna, would you believe? You can show me around. It'll be an adventure."

Pip had to agree. "If you come on the bus, I can meet you at the stop. It's outside Jelly-and-Juice, the local café. I'm not sure if it's the one that was here when we came with Big Nanna, but we can have lunch there."

"I'll be driving, not taking the bus," Jan said.

"Okay." That was probably best. The bus came through Jellico Bay at eleven o'clock on Tuesdays and Thursdays and returned at five. Six hours was a long time to spend showing her cousin around a town of nine hundred souls, only twenty or so of whom Pip knew by name.

Make that nineteen or so, now we've lost Mister Clancy.

"I really am sorry," she said.

"I know."

"If—if you ever need anyone to talk to, give me a call."

"And you'll answer your phone this time?"

"I promise I will. If I miss your call, I'll phone you straight back as soon as I realise. By the way, how did you get my —"

"Thank you." Jan sounded as if she meant it.

"Okay. Give me a call when you plan to come."

"Lupin's birthday, I thought."

That was in less than a week. So much for ten months' grace.

"Yes. Fine. See you then."

Pip's thumb hovered over the end-call button, but Jan said hastily, "Pip? I don't know your address!"

That's because I never gave it to you.

Pip felt mean and petty. Obviously, Jelly-and-Juice wasn't a suitable meeting place after all. Not in the circumstances. Anyhow, why shouldn't Jan have her address? It wasn't as if she'd be dropping in every day . . . not with a five hour round trip drive . . . or was it more? Jan hadn't lived in Delmsford for years, and Pip couldn't remember, if she'd ever known, her most recent home address.

She said, "I'm at *Lemonwood* . . . that's the name of my cottage. It's number six Ribston Lane. You'll think number five is the last one in the lane, but we're there all right — set back from the road. There's a drystone wall that hides the cottage. I'll tie a scarf around the tree where you can park in case you don't want to risk the gateway. It's pretty narrow."

"We?"

"Oh — didn't I say? I—" Pip paused. She'd almost said *I have two cats,* but that would have been untrue and ridiculous. She certainly wouldn't say *I'm owned by two cats,* because that was twee and precious.

"I?" Jan prompted.

"I live with two cats," Pip managed.

"Oh. Do you think — no, forget it. I'll see you soon."

Jan hung up.

Pip, who was always the first person to hang up on a

call . . . unless it was a creep she'd foiled with her leave-it-and-go-elsewhere trick . . . was disconcerted.

She stared at the phone for a few frustrated seconds, wanting to call Jan back.

Yet Jan had said to forget it. Whatever *it* was.

I could tell her I've read *Underbloomers*. And that I bought it new — I didn't borrow it from the library — and that I put in a pre-order for *Garterstakes* from Jonquil at *The Orange Grove*. I should have told her that.

She was still trying to persuade herself to make like a fan and gush when her phone pinged and briefly lit up with a message.

Warily, Pip touched the screen to open it.

I was going to ask if you wanted Lupin's cat. Let me know if you do.

Chapter Thirteen. Bushman's Best

Pip glanced down at her feet, expecting a sharp pain in her ankle as Kittisack made his feelings plain.

He wasn't there — probably still wherever he'd gone when he got the hump with her earlier over the phone call.

Amberjill was probably still playing with her leaf.

Pip decided this called for a family meeting.

She'd never actually had one before. Little Mum Rosie and tidy Little Dad Jon hadn't done that kind of thing.

They were long gone, and now it was time to start.

Pip made herself a new cup of tea and cut slices of cheese to lay across the Bushman's Best Biscuits. She cut slices of cheese for the cats, too.

Technically, cats couldn't digest cheese, owing to the lactose. The original cat and the back-up cat had no truck with technicalities. Their digestive systems clearly had some kind of magic.

"I have cheese," Pip called enticingly.

Kittisack arrived first, slinking long and low to the ground.

Amberjill flashed into view, minus the leaf. She may have come through the cat flap. Pip had never actually seen her do it, but then, she hadn't seen her *not* do it.

She placed a slice of cheese before each twitching nose and waited while the cats, moving in synch and ignoring one another, bit delicately into the corners.

Why are we having a family meeting? Kittisack signalled.

"It seems necessary." Pip bit into the edge of a Bushman's Best. It was billed as a cracker biscuit, but she suspected it was someone's historical hardtack recipe. Old Mister Clancy must have had iron in his strong white teeth.

It was a local product, so maybe the Jellico Bay Historical Society knew its provenance. Could it have something to do with Captain Richaud Citron?

Through the unyielding chunks of biscuit she continued, "Jan is coming to visit in a few days. That's my cousin Juniper, remember. She prefers to be called Jan."

I prefer to be called the original cat, Kittisack reminded her.

"I'll try to remember, but Kittisack is a *name*. The original cat is simply a description."

The original cat is what I am. It is my rank and my role.

"When Jan comes, will you two be here?"

Why would you ask that? The original cat sounded puzzled.

Why would we not be here? The back-up cat skewered the remains of her cheese with a careful claw.

"I thought maybe you wouldn't be."

Pip couldn't bring herself to say she wasn't absolutely sure they were real.

She *didn't* believe she was Marie Antoinette, or Edith Cavell, or Joan of Arc, but still . . . Cat-Morse . . . and appearing without a single clunk from the cat flap.

She tried to remember if they'd ever been there when Mister Clancy came for his tea and biscuits. He'd had a good grip on reality.

She couldn't remember them being in the kitchen during the Clancy conversations, but she couldn't remember them *not* being there, either.

I must try to be more observant – and not only when I'm looking at buckets.

Kittisack leaped up into her lap, levitated his front half to put a paw on each of her shoulders and bit her nose. *Is that real enough for you?*

"Ow." Pip squinted downwards.

We'll always be here, unless you don't want us to be, Amberjill put in.

That wasn't a lot of help.

Unless we have somewhere else to be. That was Kittisack, and even less help.

We are, we were, we will be. Ommmm.

Pip sighed heavily. Cat-Zen was clearly a thing. If it hadn't been before, Amberjill had just invented it.

So, what's really on your mind? The original cat leaped down.

"How did Jan know my number?"

How long have you had it?

Pip had to think about that one. "The current phone's about seven years old. I got it after the last one fell into a rock pool while I was looking for Jellico diamonds. I think a blue-ringed octopus ate it. At least, it was clasping it in a lover-like fashion, and I wasn't brave enough to dispute with it."

I should think not! Amberjill seemed shocked.

How long have you had the number, though? Kittisack persisted.

"Oh." Pip thought again. She remembered the lad at the phone shop trying to sell her that upmarket device she didn't want. She remembered emerging in triumph with a new phone that looked like the old one, and which the chastened lad had programmed with the old number when she insisted. "I think I first got the number when Little Mum was still alive. No, I'm sure I did. It was when I was living in Delmsford."

Then your mother probably gave it to her sister, just in case.

That made sense. Pip relaxed. Nothing to see here. Perfectly logical explanation.

Rose "Rosie" Pearmain and Hellebore "Helen" de Leon were as close as sisters could be. Obviously, they'd have known the family phone numbers. Obviously, they'd have passed them on to their daughters . . . except that Rosie hadn't passed them to Pip. Pip wouldn't have wanted them.

Pip's number was mostly for her mother—and of course, for Sully.

Happy now Pippin Pearmain? The original cat's signal was acid.

Pip swallowed the masticated biscuit and sighed. "Jan asked if I wanted Lupin's cat."

The cats froze. They were so still Pip expected them to stutter the way old videotape did when it was on pause.

She remembered they didn't know the context, and so she explained as briefly as she could. "Lupin is — was — Jan's elder sister, remember? She died. Jan wants to know if I want to have her cat."

She expected Amberjill to be more open to the idea, but it was Kittisack who signalled in precise Cat-Morse that he'd survived one incomer, and so another would be of little consequence. *Three cats would seem an optimum number.*

Amberjill unfroze enough to ask, *What sort of cat?*

"I don't know."

You can't expect us to welcome a strange cat without knowing something about it.

"I welcomed a strange cat. Twice."

The back-up cat stabbed her piece of cheese.

Pip turned her attention to the original cat, who usually counselled her to *tell no one.*

"What do you say, Kittisack?"

The cat shrugged his Siamese shoulders. *As you said . . . strange cats may be welcome. As I said, three cats would be a goodly number. We could form a pleasant trinity. It is correct that there should be three cats.*

Pip drew the phone towards her with one finger on the screen. She woke it up and sent a message to Jan.

Lupin's cat is welcome here.

Then she went back to eating her Bushman's Best.

CHAPTER FOURTEEN. STRAWBERRIES AND CREAM

Jan arrived earlier than Pip expected on what would have been Lupin's seventy-first birthday. She must have left home by eight o'clock, just when Pip had been sipping hot water and lemon juice after her daily battle with the sentient lemon tree. By ten past eight the discarded husk of the lemon was already trimmed and stripped on a baking tray. The pith was ready to be added to her compost pile. Things that used to take a while had become second nature to Pip.

By nine o'clock, Pip had been out the door.

Brisk walk along the beach, looking for Jellico diamonds.

Quick call at Jelly-and-Juice, post office, and home again.

Tie scarf around tree to act as a welcome flag for Jan.

Before eleven, Jan's car edged through the narrow gateway into Pip and the cats' domain and parked neatly under the spreading oak that hugged the drystone wall a bit too closely.

When Jan straightened up from the vehicle, she looked a little crushed and haggard, but Pip was glad to see she was essentially the same as she'd been at the Delmsford Flower Show. She was even wearing the same pinafore dress.

No one dressed in mourning anymore.

Pip wondered if they would hug. They had at the show.

She watched Jan's arms to see if they made an inviting gesture.

Reading body language cues was second nature — she did it all the time when she was on stage. It cut reaction time as a body-message often came a second before the cue.

Jan locked her car and turned to Pip. She had a small grey case in her left hand as well as her lavender-printed bag over her shoulder.

An overnight bag? Was she planning to stay?

Pip smiled in welcome. A hot gush of tears fought for release, and she sniffled forlornly. "Sorry."

"Don't be." Jan dropped the case and gave her a lavender-scented hug. "It's okay to be sad, Pip. I keep telling myself that."

"*I* shouldn't be."

"You should. You and I are the only peers left to cry for Lupin. She had friends and associates, but none of them is the crying type. They're all jeans or tweed skirts and brogues or inappropriate shoulder straps. Oops, that came out unkinder than I intended. Some people might find *my* clothing a little less than chic." She gave Pip a small squeeze, leaning down to do it. "What you said about us always being with you because we're family — that was exactly right." Jan stepped back, wiped her eyes with her left hand and picked up the case again. "Lovely place you have here."

"We like it. Would you like to see around the garden? It's not as big or as wonderful as Little Mum's and Aunt Helen's were, but I can introduce you to Bill the blue-tongue, and to the gooseberry bush. Mind you, it has a taste for human flesh. The sentient lemon is worse, so we'll just bow distantly in passing and touch our curly-brimmed beavers."

She hoped Jan would pick up on that ... or did distant bows and curly beavers belong more to Regency romance than to the buxom bodice-ripper?

"I would love to see around the garden, but I could murder a cup of tea."

"Let's go in, then." Pip led the way. Out of the corner of her eye she saw the back-up cat's tail disappearing under a screen of ivy by the porch.

In her sunny kitchen, Pip flipped on the kettle which was really cold only in the morning . . .and that was if Pip had not got up at three a.m. to brew a cup of tea. "Indian?" she asked.

"If you've got it."

Pip still had half a packet of strong Indian tea left over from when she used to make it for Mister Clancy. It was encased in an earthenware crock, so she supposed it would be all right.

It smelled fresh enough when she opened the cork lid of the crock.

She made a cup of that for Jan and the familiar green-gold camomile for herself.

She grew the camomile in her garden and stored her everyday supplies in a twin of the crock that housed Mister Clancy's Indian brew. The bulk of the crop was thoroughly dried and closed in an actual tea chest she'd found in the cottage.

"I got some cakes from Jelly-and-Juice. They're not cherry jam tits or coconut cones like we had at the flower show."

"They wouldn't be, unless the *LL Gina Delmsford Hawkins Kitchen Manual* has made it to Jellico Bay," Jan said.

Pip took the patisserie box out of the pantry where she'd lodged it half an hour ago when she got home. "I'm pretty sure they use *Harold Hawkins' High Tea* at Jelly-and-Juice. At least, I've seen signed copies for sale in their café condiments and fancies annex. I can make a proper lunch if you'd prefer that. An omelette or something. I have plenty of herbs and some good cheese."

She glanced about. Usually the mention of cheese brought forth a cat or so.

No cats appeared.

Jan shook her head and indicated the box. "I want whatever you have in there."

Pip lifted the lid and displayed the contents.

"*Ooh,* butterfly cakes! And . . . is that an apricot half on that tart?"

"Could be. I thought it was an egg yolk. These are the ones Jelly-and-Juice make themselves, but *these* are from a shop called Queen of Tarts in New South Wales. The Jelly-and-Juice people get them in by special order." Pip displayed the second layer of pastries. "Strawberry Hearts, Tartan Tarts and Rhubarb Valentinos this week."

Jan sighed. "These are so lush!"

"That is the perfect description." Pip picked up a Strawberry Heart and bit into it. The perfect balance of bright fruit burst onto her palate along with soft, rich shortcrust with a slightly roughened texture, the source of which she'd never identified.

Jan took an intricately patterned tartan tart. "Oh, yum! I must take some home for—" She broke off.

"For yourself," Pip said, not looking at her. She licked her fingers. "Jan, do you remember strawberries and cream?"

"Best for high days and holidays, Little Nanna Laurel always said."

"Exactly. Little Mum thought so too. So when I moved here I started a tradition. I have it every Friday. If I can't get good strawberries, I warm up a Strawberry Heart and pour the cream over that. It's a holiday in a bowl."

"That's what I call a sensible tradition," Jan mumbled through a mouthful.

"Mind you, I also eat Bushman's Best as a nostalgic penance."

Jan spluttered. "Those appalling crackers Big Pop used to eat? He said they reminded him of his time as a midshipman in the navy. Big Nanna said not even *he* was old enough to have been forced to eat those—mind, she also said they never attracted weevils."

"That's them. Mister Clancy, the one whose bucket I bought recently, used to like them. I laid in a stock of the things just before he died, so I eat one now and again so they don't go to waste. Want one?"

"Not on your life. I stand with the weevils on that. I'd rather use them to sole my shoes." Jan spluttered a laugh. "Do you remember when we took one of Big Pop's Bushman's Best and put it in a bowl? Lupin poured boiling water over it. When the water went cold — "

" — we took out the biscuit and dried it on a teacloth," Pip continued.

"Then we put it in the airing cupboard," Jan went on.

"And later, we put it back in the packet." Pip shook her head. "Did Big Pop ever notice?"

"No idea," Jan said. "If he did, he never said so." She laughed and drank her tea. "About that bucket."

"It's over there." Pip nodded towards the corner by the stove. She glanced at the grey case Jan had set down by the table beside her lavender-print shoulder bag. "Are you staying the night?"

"What? No — "

"You're welcome if you want to. The west room — " She had been about to say the west room was empty, but she recalled it certainly wasn't. It was filled with crates and boxes she'd brought when she moved from *Treasures* but never yet unpacked.

"Or there's always the couch," she ventured. "It's a good couch. I sometimes sleep there by mistake."

"I know the feeling." Jan pushed her hand through her pepper-and-salt hair. "So many women our age have trouble sleeping. I'm not one of them. Dropping off at my desk or on the couch is a frequent occurrence."

Pip nodded, acknowledging fellow feeling.

"I might take you up on that one day, but not today," Jan said.

She must have seen the direction of Pip's gaze because she

bent to lift the case. "This isn't an overnight case, if that's what you thought. It's a few things Lupin wanted you to have. She didn't want a Reading of the Will any more than she wanted a funeral. *The Last Gift* people came and packed up the things she hadn't got around to sorting out. As I said, we thought we had more time."

"Oh." Pip wondered about Lupin's cat. Should she mention it? Surely Jan hadn't left it in the car . . . oh, what if it had died of grief?

"Lupin was quite well off," Jan went on. She took an envelope from the case. "She wanted to leave you some money, so she set up a bank account. The information is in here."

Pip bit hard on her bottom lip.

Jan smiled. "You remember when we met at the flower show? You told us you planned to burst onto the scene as the Dancing Centenarian and make a fortune. You said you'd leave some of that to Lupin and me if you predeceased us."

Pip felt a surge of awfulness. "If I'd had any idea Lupin was ill I wouldn't have said that."

"Of course you wouldn't. But Lupin thought it was fun, anyway. She said this was your centenarian fund because *one* of us had to make it through a marathon of life."

"This ought to go to you and —" Her memory glitched and righted itself . . ."Clarkia."

"We're fine. Lupin said if you refused your share it was to just stay in the bank in perpetuity, enriching no one *but* the bank shareholders. She threatened to install a virtual Cerberus to savage anyone *but* you who tried to access the account."

Pip could just hear Lupin saying that.

CHAPTER FIFTEEN. OUT OF THE COBWEBS

Jan delved in the case again and took out a knobbly bundle wrapped in white tissue paper and swaddled in clear sticky tape. "This is Lupin's cat." She frowned slightly and glanced about. "Speaking of cats — where are yours? You said there were two?"

Pip had been wondering that. Apart from the vanishing tail of the back-up cat, she hadn't seen so much as a whisker since she returned from Jelly-and-Juice filled with resolve and bearing a double-layered patisserie box.

"They'll be around," she said.

Jan looked under the table. "Kitty-kitty?" She made a kissing noise. "Come on kitties . . ."

"They're probably —"

"Oh, what a gorgeous boy!" Jan bent as far as she could and stretched out her arms.

Pip, hardly believing it, ducked her head under the table.

Her startled gaze saw the cat sitting daintily at Jan's feet, offering his cheek to her outstretched fingers.

"Where did you come from?" she asked suspiciously.

"Out of the cobwebs, a piece of the sun, from thistles and velvet are kitten-cats spun," Jan quoted.

The shared memory rustled in Pip's mind. *Grandmother's Sunshine.* That book of magical rhymes, gentle stories and soft, delightful drawings . . . printed on thick cream pages Little Mum had said were made of rag and flax. Little Mum Rosie and Aunt Helen had each had a copy, inscribed in flowing brownish ink *from Grandmother Aster to her sweet Cammie* and *from Grandmother Aster to her sweet Callie.* Since these weren't Mum and Aunt Helen's names, the books must have come down to them from someone else.

Pip said, "I wish we'd asked about those books."

Jan straightened, pushed her chair back, and patted her pinafored knees. "You can come up here . . . good boy. Oh, okay, you stay down there, then." She glanced at Pip as she sat up as well. "I *did* ask about them."

"And?"

"Little Nanna Laurel said she remembered someone called Callie—she was her great-granny."

"*Und?*" Pip waited eagerly for enlightenment.

"*Und* nothing," Jan said with seeming regret. "She didn't know her very well. Little Nanna did say Callie had a sister called Cammie. There was a picture of them somewhere . . . maybe one of those old sepia photos."

"Cammie—Camilla? Cameo?"

"Camellia, maybe. Probably a plant name."

Little Nanna Laurel's first name had been Schizanthus, which Pip still couldn't spell, but that had been okay since Little Pop had always called her Anth.

"I wonder how we came to get Cammie's copy of the book," Pip mused.

"No idea . . . unless she didn't have any children. Do you still have it?"

"Of course I do." Pip was surprised that Jan felt the need to ask.

"I thought maybe you'd downsized when you moved."

"I did, but I would never get rid of any of my favourite books—especially not that one. I mean, it's not as if I could just go and buy a new copy." Of the few people Pip had mentioned *Grandmother's Sunshine* to over the decades, not one outside of her close relatives had evinced even the vaguest memory of it.

Jan said, "If you ever do want to sell it, will you let me know first?"

"Obviously." Pip felt a hot blush building in her cheeks and got up to re-boil the kettle to hide it. She rarely told a direct lie, but she *had* almost given up the lovely little book — not for money, but for love. It had been during her friendship with Alison and Angie Blake.

Angie had been such a delightful child. She and Pip shared a taste for Butterfly Princess designs, colourful clothing, and dancing. Pip fancied that Angie was the kind of child she might have borne if she'd ever taken that path. She'd given her the tin kaleidoscope, a kind of admission, to herself at least, that she would not be having a daughter.

Alison hadn't minded the kaleidoscope, although she must have known it was a vintage 1960s toy. It had come as a bitter surprise, therefore, when she'd reacted so oddly when she came upon Pip and Angie sharing the rhymes and dreamy watercolour stories of *Grandmother's Sunshine*.

Angie had been able to read a few words, and she'd handled books with fond care. Pip had felt comfortable about letting her turn the pages herself. *Grandmother's Sunshine* had survived at least three generations of the Laurel-Pearmain-de-Leon families, so why should it not survive a little Blake?

They'd been enjoying a tiny, jewel-like story about an elf child who climbed a waterfall when Alison returned with her shopping and said it was time to go home.

Angie had asked to finish the story, and Pip had said impulsively that she might borrow the book. "Mum and Dad will help you with the big words," she'd said, as much to Alison as to Angie.

That was Alison's cue to say *thank you* and that of course they'd help and that they'd take great care of Miss Pip's lovely book.

Instead, Alison had put out her hand for the book, scanned

it, and given it back to Pip with a brusque, "No thanks."

"It's okay, really. I know Angie will look after it."

"I'd rather she doesn't borrow it, Pip—kids don't always understand the difference between *mine* and *yours* as it is."

"Well then, she can have it to keep!" Pip had felt a tiny pang, but after all . . . she had no one else to give the book to. She knew the tales and verses almost by heart, and they were twined about her memories like delicate vines. When she died, eventually, the book would just—well, just go where unwanted books went. Better by far that it should go to someone who would love it as she did.

Alison's pretty face had hardened a bit and she had shaken her head before producing a neighbourly smile. "No, please. *No*, Pip. It's kind of you to offer but—no. Chad and I prefer Angie to have new books. Right, Angie-pangie? We like new things."

Pip had taken the book back, feeling snubbed, but a tiny bit relieved. "Okay. Is it all right if I buy Angie a new book instead? I'd love to give her something, because she's such a good reader already." She knew her small friend would be turning five very soon.

"Yes of course!" Alison sounded more friendly and the chill had gone from her face. "You'd like that, wouldn't you, Angie-pangie? A nice new book? Maybe you could go with Miss Pip to choose it."

The child had nodded but had cast a longing glance at *Grandmother's Sunshine*. She'd been thoroughly invested in the story of *Wayland and Lysander*.

Pip had resolved that they'd finish that story next time she minded Angie. Yes, and they'd read all the others, one by one.

Would it be very terrible of me to ask her not to mention it to her mummy?

She never *had* done that. She'd simply trusted that Angie would have the sense not to talk about a book her mother clearly didn't appreciate.

She'd pondered the situation over the years. Why *had* Alison reacted so badly to a simple children's book? The stories were old-fashioned, but there was no bloody violence and none of the attitudes or terms that made modern parents and educators so uncomfortable. Many of the characters were children, stepping up and out, adventuring, befriending and returning safely home.

The pictures were exquisite.

Why was Alison so opposed to sharing those stories with her child?

Twenty-five years after the fact, Pip still had no idea.

CHAPTER SIXTEEN. LUPIN'S CAT

Pip came back to the present with a jolt as Jan spoke. It sounded as if she was repeating a question.

"Pip? What's his name?"

What . . .

She stilled the bubbling kettle and made more tea.

"I generally call him *the original cat*," she said cautiously as she set the cups on the table. She did not use her marigold cup this time. She didn't feel she deserved it.

She hoped Jan was referring to Kittisack and not to some conversational topic she'd missed in her book-fuelled reverie.

Grandmother's Sunshine had almost enmeshed her in those bitter-sweet memories. Maybe it was a dangerous book to be lost in.

Jan said, "That's a classic Pippin Pearmain evasion. I didn't ask what you call him. I asked his name. Unless it's a secret?" She raised one brow.

"You'd better ask him that," Pip said crossly, feeling caught out.

Jan bent again and hoisted the cat into her lap. He ducked his head and purred. "So, what's your name, gorgeous boy?"

By then, Pip would barely have been surprised if the cat had answered in fluent Cat-Morse and if Jan had understood, but it didn't happen. Instead, Jan nodded intelligently as if listening. "Ah, I see."

"What do you see?" Pip asked.

"He's called Unseelie."

That sort of made sense. The original cat was a seal point,

and he was definitely unseelie at times. He was unnerving, unchancy and uncanny, too.

Jan went on stroking him. "What about the other one? You said there were two."

"I think she's under the ivy outside. She spends a lot of time on the porch."

"Right." Jan tickled the cat's whisker pads. "There you are, Unseelie. You'd better jump down now so I don't spill my tea on you."

The cat sprang down and sauntered off towards Pip's bedroom.

Jan gazed after him. "He's a treasure, and so civilised for an unneutered tommie. Wherever did you get him?"

"He came with the house," Pip said. She suppressed a shudder at the idea of someone proposing to neuter Kittisack. Blood would be shed, and it wouldn't be the original cat's.

She indicated the knobbly bundle. "Did you say *that* is Lupin's cat?"

"Yes—oh!" Jan's face crinkled into laughter as she picked up her cup. "Don't tell me you were expecting a real one?"

"You said *Lupin's cat*. That implies a real cat to me."

"I suppose I thought you knew what I meant, but I guess . . ." Jan blinked. "When Lupin was first diagnosed, she said she didn't have enough time to do a lot of things, but she *did* want to do something new. I suggested a few things I thought she'd enjoy, but she wanted it to be different and out of character. Something about the *path not taken*. So we got together and did a weekend pottery class."

"Really? *Pottery*? I can't imagine Lupin in a pinny with a wheel and covered in clay."

Lupin had never been crafty. The older generations all had some kind of creative pursuits, but in Lupin the family talent had manifested as mathematics, management and, frankly, manipulation.

Jan laughed. "Neither could I . . . We went to a historic pub in Adelaide and there were just the four of us in the class, Lupin and me, an old priest, and an extremely odd woman a bit younger than me. At least, I assume so. She was even taller than Lupin." Jan shrugged as if tossing off a memory. "The teacher was from Yorkshire, I think. He set up everything and taught us the basics and on the first night he took our models away to fire in his kiln.

"The next day we got to decorate them, then they were glazed and fired again, and at the end of the session we took them home."

"You went all the way to *Adelaide*? To make *pottery*?"

Jan looked a bit hurt.

Pip backpedalled rapidly. After all, she didn't like it when people said things like that to her . . ."No reason not to, obviously . . ."

"There *was* a good reason not to. It wasn't at all a good idea from a medical point of view, but Lupin insisted, so we went. She was so far out of her element it was almost funny." Jan put down her cup again and tapped the bundle. "Anyway, we both made ducks, because they're easy shapes, but Lupin and the priest made cats too. Lupin said I could have her duck to keep mine company, but she didn't mention the cat at the time." She chuckled. "I suspect she edited the cat out of her memory. Anyone would!"

Pip picked up the bundle. "Thank you. I'll put it — "

"On the mantelpiece," Jan suggested.

"Good idea." Pip was surprised to feel a tad disappointed. She had never previously thought of acquiring a third cat, but she'd got used to the idea over the five days since Jan's message. Kittisack and Amberjill had disparate personalities, and it might be fun to add another one to the mix.

"On the other hand, maybe it would be safer at the bottom of a well," Jan added.

Pip blinked. She tried to remember if she'd mentioned the Clancy wishing well to Jan when she'd explained the provenance of the Clancy bucket. She thought not.

CHAPTER SEVENTEEN. CAT-MUMMY

Pip had been picking at the sticky tape binding the cat-mummy for some time when Jan suggested she ought to use scissors.

That would have been a brilliant idea if she'd had any. She had clippers, and some secateurs for the garden, but these were not much use for slicing through cat-mummy wrappings.

"I've got some nail scissors somewhere," Jan said. She hunted fruitlessly through her lavender-printed shoulder bag.

"In there?" Pip indicated the small case.

"No. That's a just-for-today case. My bag is where I carry my everyday stuff. The scissors are probably in the car with the sunscreen and emergency Caraway's Comfits. How about using a knife?"

Pip got up and fetched the bread knife. She started sawing hopefully at the tape.

Jan's left hand flexed. Obviously, she was dying to have a go.

Pip said, "I could stick it in a bucket of water to dissolve the glue. Or would that dissolve Lupin's cat?"

"Nothing will dissolve Lupin's cat," Jan said. "Nick — that was the tutor — told us his materials are tough enough to withstand any normal use. He said not to throw it at a wall. No idea why. Unless . . ." She turned her eyes inward, as if thinking of something strange.

Pip felt the first layer of tape give under the blade. She

started again and sawed until she'd made a jagged cut all the way around. Then she put aside the knife and tried to peel the wrapping free. It wouldn't peel.

"Let me." Jan reached out and Pip handed her the bread knife.

She wondered why Jan had sealed it up in the first place. A towel wrapped around the thing would have worked if it needed protection. Yet, why should it, if it was as tough as the tutor suggested?

She almost asked.

Jan used the tip of the knife to make a hole and went to work peeling back tape.

Pip ate another tart, enjoying the unusual zing of rhubarb. These tarts had been new special stock for St Valentine's Day, but they were still being made, so they must be popular.

Pip put away the unworthy and all-too-frequent pang she felt when contemplating the popularity of something she liked.

Mind you, she comforted herself, if it wasn't popular enough they'd stop making it.

"Aha!" A pleased exclamation from her cousin brought Pip's attention back from fruit and pastry, just in time to see the tape-and-paper pull apart like a papier-mâché shell.

Lupin's cat had hatched, or possibly shed its cocoon.

Pip saw immediately why Jan had layered on the tissue-and-tape.

Lupin's cat was extraordinary ugly.

It was lumpy, and knobbly, and it had a crooked tail. Its green eyes squinted, one up, one down and its ears were as crimped as a Scottish fold's.

And yet . . .

Pip clasped her hands. "Oh! It's so — so — so — "

Jan regarded Lupin's cat with a disbelieving air. "I've seen this creature on a daily basis since Lupin died, but it never stops surprising me."

"Maybe you should keep it," Pip offered.

"No, thank you. Honestly, it gives me the willies. My reluctance to give it to you is all for your sake, believe me. It's so inept. And when was Lupin ever inept?" Jan looked troubled. "I can't bring myself to bin it. It's the last thing she made — the last time —" Her voice stumbled.

"Wasn't it a while ago?" Pip asked, with her entranced gaze still fixed on Lupin's cat. It niggled at her memory in a floral and diffident way.

"Not long ago at all." Jan swallowed. "We decided on the course back when Lupin got the news that there was nothing to do but wait. She wasn't *sick,* you know. Most of the time she felt reasonably normal. Normal for seventy, that is. We started to hope . . . well, *I* did . . . that the doctors had got it wrong or mixed up her test results with someone else's. It *does* happen. Do you remember when Dad went to get an x-ray and a locum was trying to tell him about his patella? There was nothing wrong with his patella. It was his scapula. In the finish, they found out the x-rays weren't for *Lance de Leon.* They were of someone called *Vance Dion.*" She laughed. "Dad didn't get much of an apology, either, for being messed about. I hoped something like that had happened to Lupin, but she said there were other tests done and they were all, in her words, *depressingly and unusually in mutual accord.*"

Jan sighed.

"We were going to make the pottery trip into a birthday celebration for Lupin, but there was a sudden cancellation vacancy two weeks early. If we'd waited . . ."

Her eyes glazed with tears.

If they'd waited, Lupin's cat would not exist.

Pip said stoutly, "I love it. I'd be honoured to have it." She picked up the pottery cat and turned it about. It was painted a pearly grey, and intricately patterned with tiny purple-blue spires of flowers, applied with a fine brush. *Lupins.*

The contrast between the awkward modelling and the delicate floral beauty of the piece delighted her. It felt *right* in her hands.

She narrowed her eyes so light seemed to spangle her lashes.

Where have I seen you, or someone like you, before?

You know.

What?

Pip almost dropped the cat but recovered herself.

Jan watched her for a few seconds before she puffed out her cheeks. "You mean that. You really want it," she said.

"I do."

"I thought you might — I hoped so. Lupin said she thought you'd react this way."

Pip, still fondling Lupin's cat, looked enquiringly at Jan. "I thought you said Lupin didn't mention who was to have her cat?" She kept her tone mild. Accusing Jan of fibbing would not only be unkind, but unpolitic, considering her own fib about never considering relinquishment of *Grandmother's Sunshine*.

"I meant she didn't say anything *then*, when she gave me the duck," Jan responded. "Sorry, Pippin. I wasn't being evasive on purpose. I had to get a genuine feeling for your reaction. The creature really does give me the willies. It's like one of those paintings with the eyes that seem to follow you around the room. I almost couldn't stop looking at it, and every time I managed I had to look again in case it was up to something behind me.

"Lupin thought that was funny. She said if you didn't want it I wasn't to feel obliged to keep it out of survivor's guilt."

Pip patted Lupin's cat on its strong nose. "It's a tommie. Does it have a name?"

"Not as far as I know." Jan folded her hands. "I don't think Lupin named it."

Pip waited. She sensed Jan had not finished with the

surprises yet.

She was right.

Chapter Eighteen. Hot Unicorn

Jan caught Pip's eye and looked uneasy.

"Do you know, Little Pippin, I've never been able to tell what you're thinking."

Pip raised an eyebrow. "Does it matter?"

"Not usually, but it would be nice to know sometimes. Is it something to do with you being an actor?"

"I never thought of it that way, and anyway I'm not an actor—exactly. More of a performer," Pip said. She added, with a mild pang of honesty, "I'm not even that nowadays. I haven't been in anything for years."

"Too many poor scripts on offer?"

"More like *no* scripts on offer. Not for me."

Jan said awkwardly, "Maybe that's because you flitted."

"Possibly. It's a good excuse, but it's also the egg to the chicken. When I noticed the work offers had dried up I could *tell* myself it was because I was hard to find. Much less humiliating than contacting Sully's heirs and assigns and checking to see if I'd fallen off their books." That was too true for comfort, so she turned the tables. "How do your publishers find *you*?"

"Easily. They type in cherrytits at junipergin dot com." Jan raised her eyebrow in a mirror image at Pip.

"Your email address is *cherrytits?* You named yourself after a *biscuit?*"

"Why not? I always liked them. It could have been worse. Could have been *cherry-titted-nibbles*, but that might have involved hyphens or underscores, and those are always bad news in a work email."

Pip laughed. "Maybe that's why I never get work emails."

"Oh?"

"Pippin underscore Pearmain at Sullivan underscore Gilbert underscore Agency dot com. If that's even still their address. Anyhow, I read your first book and I have the second one on pre-order."

"From the library, naturally," Jan said, deadpan.

"Wash out your mouth with soap. I bought *Underbloomers* online from The Orange Grove. I'd have got it locally, but Jellico Bay doesn't run to a bookshop . . . unless you count the Harold Hawkins book at Jelly-and-Juice. The people at the Grove are good about stocking all the books in a series. It works to their advantage, making them the first port of call over all those shops that persistently stock books one and two and maybe seven and also the newest. There's one particular series where book eleven is almost impossible to find. The Orange Grove has it. They reorder *before* they sell the last one in their inventory."

"I'd have given you a review copy of it if you'd asked. Maybe I should have done it anyway, but I didn't have your address and we'd been out of touch for so long and besides — it would —"

It would have looked presumptuous.

Pip grinned at her. "If you had, I'd have been officially obliged to read it."

"But you read it anyway!"

"It was recommended to me by someone who knew my taste." She didn't mention the recommendation had come from Lupin, although Jan probably guessed. "It was funny — more than that — it was witty. I liked the floral motif. And the hero's obsession with *lusty bedders*. Talk about a son of the soil!"

"Hm," Jan murmured.

"I've always thought petunias made lusty bedders."

"They do."

Pip had a flash of planting petunias with Angie Blake. They weren't her favourite flowers by any means, but they were a bright addition to a garden when everything else was running to legginess and flopping with late-summer exhaustion.

She wondered if whoever bought the Blake house enjoyed the blooms.

Angie must have been disappointed not to have seen them out in their hundred-percenter glory. They'd looked at the label which displayed three different colours and talked about probabilities and distribution and chance. Not that they'd used those terms.

Jan tucked her chin down, possibly being bashful.

Pip pulled herself out of petunia-tinted memories and said, "So your publishers and your fans can find you via the cherrytits email address. Do they know who you are in your small-town life? That's if you still live in a small town."

Her cousin picked up her cooled cup of tea and drank it before she replied. "The publishers do, of course. The fans don't. I use a sprig of juniper berries in a cocktail glass for my author picture and any promos."

"I noticed." Pip cocked her head to one side. "Jan, why the big secret? You can't possibly be embarrassed about writing a book *that* good. Our family doesn't *do* embarrassment."

"I'm not embarrassed. As you say, why should I be?"

"Then why not use your real name and image? I always do. Did. And Sully and I made sure it was up to date on my resume and show-reel, so anyone looking to cast me knew what I looked like *now*, not only way back when. It's a waste of your time and the casting people's if they're after a thirty-something and you roll up looking decidedly fifty-two."

Jan put aside her cup. "You could hardly avoid using your real image since you appear in person or on screen, and your name is perfect for you."

"My real image caught up with me. As I said, the phone stopped ringing and the parts stopped coming after Sully died, but the rot set in before that. Look at me!"

Jan looked, with a pucker between her brows. "Ja. *Und?* You're in excellent shape."

"I am. But—there are not many parts for fifty-something or sixty-something women unless they are *doyens of the screen and stage,* and dameworthy. I was always a niche performer. I don't fit the mould of a businesswoman or a matriarch or a confidante. I don't look naturally downtrodden or naturally perky or even woman-next-door. I just—"

"You look like Pippin Picotee Pearmain."

"Yes, and I always did."

Jan smiled reminiscently. "The three of us . . . remember the photos of when we were young? There was *never* any doubt about which of us was which in those."

"Six years between you and Lupin made it pretty obvious."

"Yes, but Mum had studio portraits done of Lupin and me at two years old. She dressed us in the frilly hen's bum knickers and a little smocked dress. She'd been photographed in the same outfit at the same age—Aunt Rosie too, I expect. We're in the same background and more or less the same pose—six years apart, but you wouldn't know it. Yet Lupin is *obviously* Lupin—plotting world domination—and I am obviously me, probably wondering if the photographer was really a spy in disguise or looking at the words on the lens and hoping they were part of a story. We also have a picture of you at the same age, taken in between the others. It's a different background, and you're in little dungarees and a pink shirt, but you couldn't possibly be anyone *but* Pippin Pearmain, off in your own little world. You're even on tiptoe."

"Little Nanna Laurel used to say I was *halfway to fairyland in my head.*"

Jan laughed gently. "Exactly! I got a matching portrait

done of Clarkia for Mum and Dad, but I couldn't use the same dress. It wouldn't do up on her. She was quite a bit bigger than any of us were at the same age."

"Especially me," Pip said.

"Let's face it, Pippin — was there ever a full-term singleton child smaller than you?"

Pip shrugged. "So, we look like ourselves."

"I had to put her in a modern version, and it didn't look the same at all — different fabric, for a start. Afterwards, I wondered which outfit I should use for baby number two . . . the old one and maybe take the picture earlier to make sure it would fit or the new one to match with Clarkia's. Or even do both."

Pip furrowed her brow. "Baby number two?"

"The one we intended to have," Jan said. She shrugged. "Didn't happen."

"Oh." Pip saw maybe that was venturing onto personal ground, so she switched back to an earlier part of the conversation. "What's with the juniper berries in place of your author photo, though?"

"Marketing decision. I had a few meetings with the marketing team at Hot Unicorn Press, and they told me, ever so kindly, that I didn't fit the image."

"That's ridiculous."

"That was my knee-jerk reaction too, but then I calmed down and thought it through. In life, we all choose how to present ourselves. Mostly, we try to be a slightly upmarket version of what we really are. We put on makeup, or wear a pop-tit bra, or colour our hair, or shave our legs or whatever. It's not necessarily to impress men, or other women, either. I think it's about trying to look the way we *feel* we look. We also do it to gain attention, or to make a favourable impression, or to appear right for whatever role we want, and I'm not just talking about *your* sort of roles."

Pip wanted to object, but something was stirring in her psyche. Tiny Pippin Pearmain. Fey, fairy-like, elfin, delightful, spontaneous, vibrant, joyful, enigmatic—

Good God, Pip thought. Have I been living in the image crafted for me when I was a child performer?

Jan nodded to her. "I can see you get what I mean. Remember the way Lupin dressed and styled her hair? Skirt and blouse and suitable shoes—and an Eton crop, God save us! What else could she have been but an old-school headmistress? She might have stepped right out of the pages of a book by Dimity Lawrence!

"Now, writers are a bit different. A school principal or a performer or a politician or an athlete all need to look the part. Their faces, their clothing, their physique and their body language are all part of their stock-in-trade. That's because people *see* them in their roles. Writers, though, have a choice. We can present ourselves in whatever way will sell our image and get that image to sell books. Except that some of us really can't." She tapped her chest. "I really can't. Oh, I could dress to kill, and slather on pancake or get a glamour makeover, but I will still look like me. I'll still have a broad face, sensible hair, and a figure like a bag of flour with a rope tied around it."

"I like the way you look," Pip said.

"So do I." Jan smiled. "I do! I look the way I am, and the way I feel. I look like myself. Grounded. I look like someone who will eat three tarts and a butterfly cake and enjoy them without the faintest guilt. I look—low maintenance."

Pip understood that. She considered she was low maintenance—although she allowed that might have been because she was in charge of the maintaining.

"It's a form of pride . . . even vanity," Jan went on. "If I could click my fingers and lose ten kilos, gain dewy skin and limpid blue eyes, and grow blonde hair down to my bum, I wouldn't do it. I'm vain enough to say to the world, *Take me as I am.* However, this truthful image I have is not one to sell bodice-rippers . . .and by the way, we're trying to come up with a better and more accurate term for what I write than that. Maybe *Full-Bodied Fiction.*

"I don't look sexy, or kick-arse-heroine, because I'm not. If I was ninety instead of sixty-four, or weighed one-twenty kilos instead of seventy, or had a facial scar, or rocked a police commissioner's uniform, I could sell by juxtaposition. As it is, I'm too midrange. Too average. Too ordinary. Too here's-your-granny. You could pass me a dozen times and not be able to describe me. Remember how we used to joke about the Lilac Ladies and how they must be made on an assembly line according to a paper pattern? Well, I might as well have turned into one. Put me in a pinny with the LL logo and *voila!*

"That's what the Hot Unicorn boys explained to me. Publishers are businesses, and authors produce commodities. Image helps sell. An author's name is a brand. Therefore—we do what we can to make that brand successful." She shrugged. "I was partway there already. Juniper is a really good author name. It's unusual but not weird. It's easy to spell and easy to say. Pairing it with a short, alliterative surname was a no-brainer. Juniper Gin. Someone with that name could be any age, unlike a Jan Sharman, who is likely to be in her sixties. My visual image is more difficult, as I said. The Hot Unicorn boys and I came up with the martini logo. It was either that or hire a model, and I didn't want that. They were—and are—wonderful to work with. They want me to be successful. I want to be successful. We're a team."

"What if someone wants to interview you?" Pip asked.

Jan laughed. "We discussed that. Most interviews are done online anyway, or on the phone. *If* it ever came down to a TV interview, we could play the big hat and veil card, or use heavy backlighting. It probably won't come to it, though. Have you any idea how many books are published by how many authors and how many of those get *any* media attention, or even a review that isn't a precis?"

Pip didn't, but she supposed it was something like the statistics for midrange performers. "I see."

"Yes. It's nothing to do with being embarrassed, or ashamed of what I do. I don't care what the neighbours think. I don't use real people in my stories and so there's no way anyone will be offended — unless they choose to be. If there's one thing I've picked up in life it's that some people *always* choose to be offended."

"Then what was that routine you and Lupin did at the flower show?" Pip put down Lupin's cat and mimed the bodice-ripping act she remembered. "She dropped threatening hints and you *cringed*."

Jan leaned forwards. "We were playing with you. Having fun. God knows, we needed some fun, and you made a perfect audience for our little routine."

"I see." Pip thought she'd absorbed as much candour as she could for the moment. "Would you like to see the garden now?"

Jan looked mildly taken aback at the abrupt change of subject but indicated that she would.

CHAPTER NINETEEN. PERSONAL USE

Pip felt oddly unwilling to leave Lupin's cat behind in the kitchen, but she thought carrying it about the garden like a mediaeval saint on progress might be a bit too odd, even for her.

It might also be playing into her image.

After Jan's spiel, she felt rocked and unbalanced.

She cast a glance at the framed embroidery of a ducks and river scene she had hung in her minute hall. Little Nanna Pearmain had been working on that in her last days. She hadn't quite managed to finish it, but Little Dad had reassured her it would be done, and so it was. The proof of Little Dad's filial devotion hung on Pip's wall.

What other man would learn to embroider in a week to honour a promise to his mum?

I didn't honour my promise to my mum. It was an implied one, but still, I should have done it.

As they passed the porch swing, the back-up cat phased into view in its seat like the Cheshire Cat in reverse.

Pip, distracted from her sober thoughts, hoped Jan hadn't noticed, but the odd *glerk*ing sound her cousin made suggested she had.

Okay, so now Jan was feeling unbalanced.

Serve her right.

Pip bit the bullet. "This is the back-up cat." She picked up the calico and displayed her to Jan.

Jan made a speedy recovery. "I bet her name's *Forever Autumn*."

"That would suit her but actually . . . Her name is Amberjill."

The back-up cat froze as she had when the subject of Lupin's cat was first mooted.

Pip said, apologetically, "Back-up cat, this is my cousin, Juniper Gin, Jan Sharman, or Cherry Tits. We've been sharing secrets, so I thought we'd bring you into the loop. You can be First Queen in the reshuffled pack."

The back-up cat relaxed and made a gentle chirrup.

Jan stopped looking spooked and looked enchanted instead. "She's gorgeous," she said to Pip. "Queen of Diamonds, right? She must be wealthy to have such opulent fur."

Amberjill Cat-Morsed pleasure at the compliment, then asked, *Where is Lupin's cat?*

"In the kitchen, but there's no need to be troubled. It's made of pottery," Pip said.

I wasn't troubled.

"You were." Pip rubbed under the ridge of the back-up cat's jaw and set her back on the swing. "Go and chase your leaf."

They continued down the porch steps, and Pip waited to see what Jan would say about that one-sided conversation.

"Is that your blue-tongue?" Jan jumped right over the verbal minefield and indicated Bill, who rested half in and half out of the woodpile.

"That's Bill. *Billardiera longifloria*, really. He's not mine, though. He came with the house." She indicated the water tank. "Watch out for the gooseberry. It will bite you if it can. The lemon tree near it is a champion at *squirt you in the eye*. I do battle with it every morning. And *there's* the Clancy wishing well."

Jan leaned in to look. "This is wonderful."

"I know. Over there is my fernery, and I have thrift and marjoram and —"

Jan's eyes bugged as she took in the forest of German

camomile, still in stalwart bloom, despite the encroaching autumn. "Glory! You can't possibly claim all that as personal use, Pip. Are you running some kind of tea empire?"

"I drink most of it," Pip said. She'd never thought of selling it.

"Ugh." Jan grimaced. "It tastes like perfume with old apples in it."

"I know. I like it."

And is that another affectation of Tiny Pippin Pearmain?

She put the thought away. Jan had left the subject behind, and so should she.

They squabbled amiably about beverages until Jan's phone chimed. She took it out of her pinafore pocket and read the message.

"Clarkia," she said to Pip. She thumbed a quick reply, which elicited another ping.

"I'll have to ring her. Texting makes my thumb hurt," Jan said, inspecting that digit. "Mild arthritis."

Pip nodded and returned to the kitchen to give her cousin some privacy. *She* didn't have arthritis — yet. She put that good fortune down to her ballet practice and strawberries and cream.

On the way, she looked for the back-up cat, but the porch was untenanted.

"Amberjill? Kittisack?"

In here, the cats signalled in chorus.

Pip entered the kitchen to find them perched on the scrubbed pine table, forming a triskele with Lupin's cat.

We like him, the original cat announced, flickering his tail.

The back-up cat sniffed delicately. *Charmed by a guardian. A rare treasure.*

"What?"

The cats purred.

A *frisson* chattered down Pip's spine. She liked being fey and a wee bit *other,* but this unexpected teaming up of the cat and the back-up cat made her uneasy. Usually they ignored one another.

Am I the sort of person who imagines conversational cats into being?

Kittisack pinned back his left-cheek whiskers and deliberately swiped them along Lupin's cat.

"Don't break it!" Pip put out a hand to the rescue.

The cat signalled creepy laughter.

You'll never break him. The back-up cat sounded almost— awed.

Chapter Twenty. Duty to the Family

Pip was still gazing at the three-cat communion when Jan came in.

She glanced at the cats—or Pip supposed she did—and must have elected not to see them. "Pip, may I use your loo?"

"Through there," Pip said, mesmerised by the cats. She supposed she should have indicated the loo already. Jan had drunk two large cups of Indian tea. Pip knew from experience that post-menopausal bladders lost some elasticity.

Jan went to the bathroom. After a bit the cistern flushed and water ran—briefly, as Pip noted with a sliver of relief. It had been a warm summer and the tank wasn't bottomless.

Jan came out with a few dark splotches on her pinafore bib, suggesting she might have splashed her face to cool it. "I'd better get going. Clarkia's coming up."

Here . . . um . . .

"To my place," Jan clarified.

"Of course." Pip knew a visiting daughter would always take precedence over a visit to a cousin. That was right. She would have thought the same as Jan if she'd been the one with a daughter.

What would I have called her if I'd had one?

It was an old occasional puzzle.

Camomile. Cammie for short. I wonder if that was what the other Cammie was really called. Or maybe Marigold. Or Eve, after the apple.

It was too late for her to have a daughter, Camomile or

otherwise. It was about — Pip checked her mental calendar. It was *at least* twenty years too late, she concluded.

I could always adopt.

You could not. No adoption agency would consider you *a suitable parent.* You *probably wouldn't consider yourself a suitable parent.*

She turned to assure Jan it was fine.

It *was* fine. She'd had about as much emotion, revelation and information as she could handle.

"Do you want to take the Clancy bucket now?" she enquired.

"Yes. I'll need it tomorrow." Jan was frowning.

Pip fetched the Clancy bucket. "I'll send you the recipe for bucket oil," she volunteered.

Jan didn't question that. She seemed to be thinking of something else, maybe seeking the future. Was she looking forward to seeing her daughter? She'd divorced herself from her visit to Pip already.

"Where does Clarkia live?" Pip asked.

"Mm? Oh — down at South East Cape."

Pip nodded, resolving to look it up later.

Jan added, "I don't see much of her, unfortunately."

"Does she have any children?" Pip thought she probably knew the answer to that. If Jan had had a grandchild, she would surely have mentioned it. She'd make a lovely nanna, having had three to use as templates. Little Nanna Pearmain was, strictly speaking, Pip's alone, but Lupin and Jan had been generous about sharing Big Nanna de Leon. In effect, the three had enjoyed the benefits of six grandparents who loved them almost interchangeably.

"Not as far as I know," Jan said. "I guess she might have fitted one in. I haven't seen her in six months, so she could have had one by now and I'd be none the wiser."

Pip could tell she didn't believe that. She said, "We didn't really do our duty to the family, did we. Genetically

123

speaking."

"Indeed not," Jan said in a dry tone. She added, "Maybe it's as well. *Look* at us, Pippin Pearmain! You, me, and Lupin. Would we really want to unleash more of our genes on the unsuspecting world?"

Pip gave it some thought. "Yes."

"What?"

"Yes. I wish we had. We were *worth* unleashing —"

"We were. We are. I was just being chicken-hearted," Jan agreed quietly. "The thing is, that even if we do our duty, as you put it, we can't be sure the next generations will do theirs."

"The first Queen Elizabeth had no children," Pip said, remembering.

Jan nodded in agreement. "Shakespeare had three. His son Hamnet died as a child. Susanna had one daughter, who died childless. Hamnet's twin, Judith, had three sons who all died without issue." She shrugged. "Same deal with the Bronte family. There were six of them, and only Charlotte married. She died a few months later — probably of pregnancy-related complications. Considering those were the days of no reliable contraception but also of high child and maternal mortality, it's all too easy to see how families can die out. Forget it."

She gave her head a sharp shake, as if to dispose of the subject.

"Would you like to read my new book when I finish the manuscript? It's called *The Root of the Matter*. You could be my beta reader."

About to refuse tactfully, Pip realised she didn't want to. "Yes please," she said.

"Good." Jan twitched a smile. "At least you won't send it back covered in metaphorical red pen the way Lupin does. Did."

"No." Pip waited a beat. "It will be green pen in my case,

in edits so small you can take off your specs and pretend they're not there." She added, "If I ever want to relinquish *Grandmother's Sunshine* in the future, I will send it directly to you. Unless you'd like it now?"

Jan laughed. "Heavens no! I don't want it. I'd just like to keep it in the family, such as it is, rather than see it go to a stranger in an op-shop."

"In case Clarkia ever has a between-visits baby."

"Oh, Pip." Jan grabbed Pip in a hug, lifting her off her feet and enveloping her in the nostalgic perfume of Caraway's Lavender Lotion. She put Pip down and backed away, stopping by her chair and becoming rapidly burdened with bag, case, and the Clancy bucket. "I'll be in touch, promise. Bye, Unseelie. Bye, Autumn."

She was out the door almost before Pip knew it.

Pip stood on the porch until Jan's car, a sensible station wagon, had slid through the narrow gateway in the wall and vanished.

Then she returned to her kitchen.

Lupin's cat occupied the table, resting in solitary state among the crumbs of butterfly cakes and tarts that had been whole five minutes ago.

Pip absolved it of eating them, putting the blame where it belonged.

"Cats, I have a bone to pick with you."

She heard a Cat-Morsed snigger from the porch. It sounded like Kittisack.

About the Author

Lark Westerly loves writing series where characters weave in and out of one another's stories.

She also loves playing with ideas and notions and researching odd information.

Lark lives in the island state of Tasmania, where she walks dogs, invents recipes, and goes around in clothes with that lived-in look. She rarely finds a matching pair of socks.

Unlike Pippin Pearmain, Lark is not tiny, not an only child, not single and not an on-screen performer. She never learned ballet and she can't speak Cat-Morse. She doesn't even have a bucket list. Nevertheless, Pippin Pearmain and Lark Westerly are sisters under the skin.

Oh . . . you were wondering about that bucket that inspired *Performing Pippin Pearmain*? It happened like this . . .

To find out, visit http://www.performingpippinpearmain.weebly.com and click on *About the Bucket List.*